"Happy N

He pressed a kiss to Amanda's forehead. Their eyes met and something arced between them. When their lips touched, he couldn't say who initiated it, but it no longer mattered. The energy flowed both ways, feeding on itself. And still the only point of contact was their mouths. That changed.

When at last he raised his head, she yanked his shirt up and off him, leaving his torso bare. She slid her hands down his back to his buttocks and pulled him hard against her, kissing him hungrily.

Dangerously close to stripping off her pajama bottoms and taking her right then and there, Nick forced himself to pull back, trembling with the effort. "Amanda, honey," he said, "we have to stop."

"No, we don't. Nick, I want to make love with you."

Gently he touched her lips and with a teasing smile said, "Aren't you the lady with the unfortunate habit of marrying any man she sleeps with?"

Dear Reader,

When four romantically minded high school girls vow to find each other husbands if any of them are still single at age thirty, they have no idea how complicated it will make their lives twelve years later! I'm giving each of our matchmaking pals—Raven, Charli, Sunny and Amanda—her own story, one each month, in THE WEDDING RING Temptation miniseries.

In *Fiancé for Hire*, two-time divorcée Amanda is determined to remain single, while her matchmaking pals are just as determined to set her up with Mr. Right. In true take-charge style, Amanda concocts a devious scheme to throw them off the scent: a phony fiancé!

THE WEDDING RING matchmaking pact was set into motion in December 2000 with *Love's Funny That Way*, when Raven Muldoon fell in love with the brother of the man her pals had chosen as her future husband. In January, Charli entered into a marriage of convenience that became decidedly inconvenient when she fell in love with her husband in *I Do, But Here's the Catch*. February gave you Sunny's story in *One Eager Bride To Go*, when a devastating secret threatened the happiness of reunited high school sweethearts.

I hope you'll join me for all four of these fun, sexy WEDDING RING stories. You can visit me on the Web at www.pamelaburford.com, or write to me (include an SASE) at P.O. Box 1321, North Baldwin, NY 11510-0721.

Love,

Pamela Burford

FIANCÉ FOR HIRE
Pamela Burford

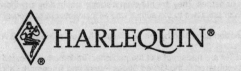

HARLEQUIN®

TORONTO • NEW YORK • LONDON
AMSTERDAM • PARIS • SYDNEY • HAMBURG
STOCKHOLM • ATHENS • TOKYO • MILAN • MADRID
PRAGUE • WARSAW • BUDAPEST • AUCKLAND

To my sister Janice Burford, with love

ISBN 0-373-25924-7

FIANCÉ FOR HIRE

Copyright © 2001 by Pamela Burford Loeser.

This edition published by arrangement with Harlequin Books S.A.

Visit us at www.eHarlequin.com

Printed in U.S.A.

1

AMANDA COPPERSMITH LOVED being The Boss.

The thought came to her unexpectedly as she exited a meeting with her art director and strolled past her assistant editors' cubicles, nodding at the deferential greetings tossed her way, pausing briefly to chat with the new copy editor and see how she was settling in.

Not that the corner office had been Amanda's conscious goal eight years ago when she'd walked out of Cornell University with a degree in journalism and the proverbial fire in her belly to do something special with it. Still, it had been a part of her even then: an entrepreneurial spark that had never let her settle for punching someone else's time clock.

Which she'd done for five years, working for various magazines, involving herself in every aspect of the business—editorial, sales, art, layout, everything. Soaking up knowledge and experience. Preparing for the day when she'd finally break out and launch her own publication.

Grasshopper.

An unprepossessing name for an entity that had come to mean everything to Amanda, in the three short years since the first issue saw print. To others, *Grasshopper* was a slick children's nature monthly, a

remarkably successful upstart in the juvenile maga-
zine market. To Amanda, it was tangible proof of her
own talent, intelligence, resourcefulness and perse-
verance.

She opened the door to her office—yes, a corner office, a spacious, sun-washed, elegantly appointed corner office, to be precise, located on the tenth floor of a
building on West Twentieth Street in Manhattan. To
her surprise, three women sat waiting for her. One
had had the temerity to park herself behind Amanda's
glass-topped desk.

"Get out of my chair, Sunny."

"I like it here." Sunny Bleecker Larsen spun the bur-
gundy leather executive chair in a circle. "Mind if I
steal this? It's more comfy than that old recliner Kirk's
folks gave us."

Amanda crossed to the sleek, blond-wood credenza
set under the picture windows in the corner. She
propped her hip on the credenza, causing the short
skirt of her tailored seafoam-green suit to ride up even
higher. She glanced at her slim gold watch. Nearly
five-thirty. "What are you guys doing in the city? You
didn't come in to go shopping, did you? Isn't this a
school day?" She looked at Carlotta "Charli" Rossi
Sterling, who taught instrumental music at their old
high school on Long Island.

"School's out for Columbus Day." Charli leaned
back in one of the two ultramodern leather guest
chairs set in front of Amanda's desk.

Raven Muldoon Radley occupied the other one.
Four and a half months pregnant, Raven had recently

begun wearing the maternity clothes Amanda had helped her pick out. Today it was a calf-length, rayon challis dress in shades of dusty blue. The color complemented her chin-length, honey-colored hair, several shades darker than Amanda's own light blond mane. Today Amanda had secured the straight, pale, shoulder-length strands in a French twist.

"I canceled my hypnotherapy clients for today," Raven said, "and Sunny got Kirk's parents to watch Ian for her. Girls' day out. Museum of Modern Art. High tea at the Plaza."

"And last but not least—" Sunny pointed a finger at Amanda "—ambushing you here at quitting time."

"I can't go to dinner with you," Amanda said. "I've got to be home by seven-thirty to let in the electrician—I'm having directional lighting installed in the kitchen. Remember?" She knew she'd mentioned it to Sunny—it must have slipped her friend's mind.

A fifteen-minute taxi ride to Pennsylvania Station, plus nearly an hour on the Long Island Railroad and the ten-minute drive to her house meant she had to leave the office by six, latest.

"Dinner isn't what this is about," Raven said.

Charli pushed her long, dark brown hair behind her ear. "We just want to talk."

"About...?" The instant Amanda asked, she knew. "Oh no. We settled this."

"That's right," Sunny said. "We settled it twelve years ago."

"When we made our pact," Raven said.

"Our solemn vow," Charli added.

"We were kids then!" Amanda rose from the credenza. "You can't hold me to a decision I made when I was eighteen. Not about something this important."

"The rest of us were held to it," Sunny pointed out. "With excellent results, I might add. Three for three."

"Now it's your turn," Charli said.

"I already told you guys, I don't want a turn. I refuse to participate. This whole wacky scheme worked for you all, and I'm happy it did—hell, I'm *thrilled* for you—but it isn't the same for me."

"You entered into this pact of your own free will," Raven said, "just like the rest of us."

"And you turned thirty on Saturday, two days ago." Charli gave a brisk nod. "Time to set things in motion."

"You're neglecting one crucial fact." Amanda gesticulated broadly. *"I don't want to get married!"*

Sunny dismissed this statement with a wave of her hand. "That's irrelevant."

"How can it be irrelevant? My God, it couldn't be more relevant! We instituted the Wedding Ring back when we were boy-crazy adolescents who thought we knew what love and marriage were all about. Well, I found out what they were about—*twice!* Two doomed walks down the aisle were more than enough to teach me that the holy state of matrimony and I don't mix."

The Wedding Ring was what the four best friends called themselves, a name they'd coined shortly after graduating high school. Under the terms of the Wedding Ring pact, if any of them reached the age of thirty unmarried, the other three would find her a husband.

There were two rules: first, the lucky fellow must not be told he was involved in a matchmaking scheme, at least not before the wedding. And second, the Wedding Ring member had to go out with the chosen man for three months, no matter what—unless he broke it off before then. The idea was that your best friends in the world, who'd known you since kindergarten, knew what—and who—was best for you, even if you didn't.

And the pact had worked three times so far, even if there had been a few glitches along the way. In March, Raven had married Hunter Radley, who happened to be the *brother* of the man her Wedding Ring pals had chosen for her.

Three months later, Charli and Grant Sterling had tied the knot—for the second time. Their first wedding, a private civil ceremony, had been part of a marriage of convenience that had turned decidedly inconvenient when the bride and groom actually fell in love with each other. In July, Charli and Grant had pulled out the stops with a big church wedding that celebrated their newfound devotion and commitment.

And just yesterday Sunny had married her high school sweetheart, Kirk Larsen, a widower with an adorable toddler named Ian. A physics professor at a local university, Kirk couldn't take time off for a honeymoon now, in early October, with the semester just a few weeks along. He and Sunny would wait until school let out for intersession in February, when they planned to soak up the sun in Cancún.

"I told you yesterday," Amanda said, "but I see it

bears repeating. I will not cooperate in any way if you attempt to set me up with a man. You guys could avoid a lot of awkwardness and embarrassment for everyone if you'd just get that through your amazingly thick skulls."

"But you agreed." Charli's expression was set. Of the four of them, she took the Wedding Ring pact most to heart—but then, back when they'd made it, Charli had considered herself plain and unmarriageable. She must have seen their girlhood promise to find one another husbands as her only chance at marital bliss. "We just want you to be happy, Amanda. I think you're lonely and you just haven't met the right man. And now you've stopped trying, after that last lousy divorce. Even your brother thinks this antimarriage routine of yours is a smoke screen to save yourself more hurt."

"My brother?" Amanda frowned. "When did you talk to Jared?"

Charli's dark brown eyes grew wide. "Uh..."

Sunny exchanged an indecipherable look with Raven. "They chatted yesterday, at my wedding," Sunny said. "Isn't that right, Charli?"

"Yes," Charli hurriedly agreed. "Yes, at the wedding."

What was that about? Amanda wondered. "You guys have some trick up your sleeve, don't you?"

Raven blinked. "Trick?"

"Don't give me that innocent act. What are you up to?"

"You know," Sunny said, "you have a suspicious mind. All we want is to ensure your happiness—"

"Is Jared in on it?" Amanda demanded. "That's a violation of the Wedding Ring rules, if he is. No outsiders are supposed to know about the pact." Only Hunter, Grant and Kirk—the Wedding Ring husbands—now knew about it, as well as Charli's grandmother, who was a much-loved confidante to all four friends. "Have you gotten my brother involved in whatever little scheme you've cooked up?"

Raven said, "You're the one with the devious mind, Amanda. That naturally leads you to suspect others of the same thing."

"You're a *hypno*therapist," Amanda said, "not a psychotherapist, so spare me the armchair analysis."

Sunny turned to Raven. "Hey, there's an idea. Maybe you could hypnotize her into fulfilling her obligation to the Wedding Ring."

"My *obligation!* Oh, I like that. It's *my* future that's at stake!"

Raven ignored her outburst. "We already have someone in mind. I just know you two will hit it off."

"Now, wait a—"

"His name is James Selden. He's a golfing buddy of Grant's—a hunky real estate developer looking for Mrs. Right. We'll bring him to your birthday party," Sunny added.

"What birthday party?" This was going too fast for Amanda. "I told you not to bother with a party for me."

"Oh. Okay," Sunny said, deadpan, as if such an order would ever be obeyed.

"The party's this Saturday," Charli said. "Eight o'clock, at my house. I hope you don't have plans for then."

"If she does, she'll cancel them," Sunny said.

"All right." Amanda knew how to pick her battles. "I'll be there. And thank you—it's sweet of you to do that for me. But no matchmaking. If you drag this James guy there for me to meet, I swear to God I'll walk right out."

Raven sighed. "Won't you just give him a chance?"

"No."

Charli said, "Don't be stubborn. How do you know you won't like him?"

"That's not the point. I've sworn off marriage. When I go out with men nowadays, it's strictly for fun. No strings."

Amanda was unmoved by her pals' protestations of innocence. They had to know she had no intention of taking up with this James Selden—or any other marriage-minded man. Raven, Sunny and Charli had concocted some sort of plot to get around her resistance; she could practically smell it. Somehow, she had to beat them at their own game.

Raven was right about one thing. Amanda *was* devious—in the best sense of the word, of course. After all, she hadn't gotten where she was by giving in and doing things other people's way. Surely a clever, determined woman like her could come up with a way to make an end run around her matchmaking friends.

As her mind massaged the problem, the germ of an idea took root.

Amanda settled back on the credenza, arms folded. "Let me ask you something. Let's say I met a man I liked, and we decided to date exclusively. If such a thing were to happen, wouldn't that satisfy my *obligation* to the Wedding Ring?"

"Not so fast." Sunny held up a hand. "The rule is three months. You have to see him for three months."

Amanda sighed. "Three months, then."

"Wait a minute," Raven said. "It's not enough for her to just date a guy for three months."

"Raven's right," Charli stated. "The whole point of the Wedding Ring is marriage, not just dating. Amanda would have to marry the man."

"That's not fair!" Amanda cried. "The rule is I have to *date* the man for three months—whether or not it leads to a wedding."

"That would be true," Sunny pointed out, "*if* you were introduced by the other members of the Wedding Ring. If the man is someone you come up with on your own—" she shrugged "—then the rules are stricter. Otherwise, who knows what you'd try to get away with."

"Well, we all know what she'd try to get away with," Raven said. "That's why it has to end in marriage."

Amanda's eyes narrowed as her quick mind rolled this around. "Okay, how about this. I date someone, we fall in love, we become engaged. Engagements sometimes fall through. As long as we're together for the magical three months, wedding or no wedding, I'm off the hook."

"I don't like this negotiating," Charli said. "This should be about love and romance. Listen to you. It sounds like you're buying a used car."

"What it sounds like to me," Raven told Amanda, one eyebrow raised, "is that you're devising a way to wriggle out of the pact. Any engagement has to be sincere. If we even suspect it's a put-on—"

"You don't really think I'd do something like that?" Amanda plastered on her most guileless expression. "I mean, come on. Even if I were to try such a lame move, let's face it. The three of you have known me practically my whole life. I'd never get away with it. I'm just not that good an actress."

Her friends seemed to ponder this. "Well," Sunny said at last, "it's okay by me, I guess. Three months and an honest-to-God engagement. But I think we're all wasting our breath. Amanda keeps saying she doesn't want anything permanent. So there won't be any special guy, any engagement—if we leave it up to her. So we're back to square one."

"Oh, I don't know." Amanda shrugged. "Maybe it's like you say. Maybe I just haven't met the right man."

"When you do," Charli said, "it'll make all the difference. Then you'll wonder how you ever could have fought the idea."

Charli was so candidly, painfully sincere, Amanda felt a pang of guilt for what she was planning to do. She truly was thrilled that her best friends had found the men they were meant to share their lives with, but she wished they could understand why their version of happily ever after just couldn't work for her.

Amanda Coppersmith hadn't failed at much that she'd set her mind to, but bitter experience had driven home one irrefutable fact: she made a lousy wife. She might have been able to convince herself otherwise if it had only been one husband who'd walked out on her, but two?

Amanda had plenty of practice concealing her feelings behind a neutral facade. She was certain that even these close friends who'd known her for a quarter of a century were oblivious to the grim direction of her thoughts.

She'd lied: she *was* a good enough actress to fool them. She'd done it before, when she'd suffered a debilitating depression during her second divorce last year. She'd do it again, to ensure there wouldn't be a third.

She checked her watch once more. "I hate to kick you guys out, but I really do have to run."

Her friends gathered their things and accompanied Amanda down the elevator and outside the building, where she automatically began scanning the street for a taxi. The sidewalk was congested with pedestrians as the surrounding offices' disgorged workers headed home. This area of the city was thick with modeling agencies and photo studios, and more than a few "dot-coms," up-and-coming Internet companies.

Amanda asked, "How long do you suppose it'll take us to get a cab? Well, at least it's not raining."

"You're on your own." Raven slung her purse strap

over her shoulder. "We're going to catch dinner at that new Vietnamese restaurant around the corner."

Amanda mock-pouted. "Without me?" she teased, stepping off the curb and wagging her arm as she spied a yellow cab with its rooftop license number glowing, meaning it was available. What luck! Usually she walked over to Sixth Avenue to hail a taxi, since traffic on Sixth headed north, in the direction of Pennsylvania Station. Catching a cab here on Twentieth, an eastbound crosstown street, meant a longer, more circuitous, more expensive ride, but she wasn't about to complain about snagging a taxi within seconds at rush hour. If she exercised enough New York assertiveness, no one else would beat her to this one. She stepped farther into the street, raised two fingers to her mouth and emitted a piercing whistle.

Yes! she thought, as the cab pulled to a stop next to her. This was a good omen. Already things were going her way!

"Enjoy your dinner," she called to her pals as she tossed her briefcase onto the back seat and slid in after it. "Penn Station," she instructed the driver. He started the meter and merged with traffic. A recorded announcement reminded her to buckle up. This time the celebrity voice belonged to Walt Frazier, onetime basketball player for the New York Knicks.

Amanda chewed over the logistics of her fledgling plan as the taxi turned right on Fifth. The guy mustn't be anyone her friends knew. He had to be some anonymous fellow she could introduce as her new beau,

get engaged to in short order and dump once the req-
uisite three months were up.

And he had to be believable, someone her pals
could imagine her falling for.

The driver interrupted her thoughts. "Con Ed's got
the street torn up on Nineteenth. I'm going to have to
go down to Seventeenth to head west."

Well, that was different—a New York taxi driver
who spoke unaccented English. He was warning her
that he'd have to drive even farther out of the way before heading north and west.

"I don't care," she said, "as long as I make my
train."

"When's your train?"

"Six-seventeen."

"No problem. I'll get you there with time to spare."

Amanda looked at the driver for the first time. He
was youngish, with short, dark hair and impenetrable
sunglasses. He wore a black T-shirt, which stretched
over lovely twitching biceps as he turned the wheel
with skill and confidence, dodging bicyclists and hap-
less pedestrians, outracing red lights, maneuvering
the car expertly through the surrounding traffic.

She settled against the worn vinyl upholstery, mull-
ing over her options. She had to move fast, a preemp-
tive strike. If she waited too long, her Wedding Ring
pals would set whatever scheme they'd concocted into
motion and she'd be left trying to play catch-up.

The cabbie glanced in the rearview mirror. Even
though he was wearing dark shades, Amanda knew

he was looking at her. A prickle of awareness raced over her skin.

"You all right?" he asked.

"What? Yes, of course." After a moment she said, "Why?"

His broad shoulders lifted and lowered. "You were kind of muttering to yourself. And you had this look on your face like a spring was poking you right through the seat."

Amanda smiled. She couldn't help herself. Normally she avoided conversation with taxi drivers, but this fellow was so personable, without being pushy or, worse, leering. She felt herself begin to relax.

"I've got a conundrum," she said, and immediately wondered if he knew what the word meant. "That is, I'm trying to solve a—"

"Work or love?" he asked, with another glance in the rearview mirror. "Or family? Whatever you're puzzling over, chances are it's one of those three."

Well, well. Not only could this taxi driver converse in the Queen's English, he possessed a respectable vocabulary. Clearly he dwelled at the top of the cabbie food chain.

Amanda checked out the hack license mounted behind the driver's head. His name was Nikolaos Stephanos. Of Greek extraction, then. She squinted at the accompanying photo, too small and blurry to tell her much, except that Nikolaos Stephanos didn't smile for license photos.

"I'm not trying to pry," he said, when she didn't respond.

"Sure you are. And since you ask, it's about love. Well, not really. It's about well-meaning friends who don't know when to butt the hell out of other people's lives."

In the rearview mirror she saw Nikolaos Stephanos grin, saw the flash of straight white teeth, in startling contrast to his swarthy skin. And was that a dimple? Oh my. If all New York cabdrivers looked this good, and smelled this good—she inhaled deeply of the clean masculine scent that drifted into the back seat— no woman would ever take the subway.

"So, what?" he asked. "Your friends have their own ideas about who you should be with?"

"Something like that." Amanda chewed her lip, while her fertile imagination took an unexpected detour.

Nah...he's a taxi driver, for heaven's sake!

"Why do people always think they know you better than you know yourself?" he asked, as he turned right off Seventeenth onto Eighth Avenue. "Reminds me of something the Earl of Chesterfield once wrote. Let me see if I remember this right. 'In matters of religion and matrimony I never give any advice; because I will not have anybody's torments in this world or the next laid to my charge.'"

Good Lord, the man quotes dead earls! Amanda peered at the hack license again. Yep, Mr. Stephanos was indeed a genuine, honest-to-God New York City taxi driver.

And an accomplished one, judging by the swift progress they were making up Eighth. Too swift, even for a quick-thinking woman of action like Amanda. She needed time to ruminate on this some more—time she didn't have.

Amanda scooted forward on the seat. "Um, this may seem like a strange question, but...have you ever done any acting?"

He glanced at her again in the mirror, only now his dark eyebrows were pulled together in a frown. "A little, in high school. Why?"

It would have to do. "Listen, I don't want you to think I'm coming on to you or anything, but if you're interested in earning a nice chunk of change, I have a proposition I'd like you to consider."

The thick silence lasted only a few seconds, but it seemed an eternity to Amanda. He asked, "What are we talking about here? Something...?" He took his right hand off the steering wheel and made a rocking gesture, which Amanda interpreted as a reference to nefarious activities.

"No!" she said. "Nothing illegal. Nothing...weird or...whatever it is you're thinking."

He waited.

She swallowed. "I want you to pretend to be my boyfriend."

"Your boyfriend."

"Yeah, it's these friends of mine."

"The ones who can't keep their noses out of your business."

"Right. Exactly. See, the thing is, if I act like I have a serious relationship with a man, then they'll leave me alone. They'll stop trying to run my life."

"What makes you think so?"

Amanda wasn't going to tell him about the Wedding Ring. She might be engaging in subterfuge to defeat the pact she'd agreed to so long ago, but it was still, well, a sacred vow, a solemn promise made to her best friends in the world. And one of the rules was you don't let outsiders in on it.

"Trust me," she said. "They'll back off."

She spotted a street sign. Thirty-first. They were almost there.

"So what's the deal?" he asked. "Are you a lesbian?"

"*What?* What makes you say that?"

"Well, this whole charade with the fake boyfriend. You're a very attractive woman," he said matter-of-factly. "It's not like you can't get a man. So I figure maybe you're just not ready to come out of the closet."

"Well, you're wrong." Amanda drew herself up, though the "very attractive" remark took a bit of the sting out of his outrageous speculation. "It's nothing like that."

"How much money are we talking about?"

"Um...well, I'd need you for three months."

"Why three months?"

"Never mind, that's how long it has to be. Like a part-time job. Weekends mainly. Double dates, that sort of thing. So my friends can see us together. Getting serious. Getting, um, engaged."

She expected another frown, but instead he laughed.

Her face heated. Damn it—she never blushed! "An

engagement in name only, needless to say. How about a flat fee of, say, a thousand dollars?"

"Let's see...three months—call it thirteen weeks. An average of two 'dates' a week, four hours per date." With barely a pause, he added, "That comes to a hundred four hours, at an hourly rate of nine dollars and sixty-two cents. Correct?"

"Uh...correct. That's what I came up with, too." Amanda resisted the urge to haul her calculator out of her briefcase and verify his math. "Is that acceptable?"

"Off the books, tax-free? No heavy lifting?" He shrugged. "I've had worse jobs."

"Is that a yes?"

"That's a yes, boss."

"Oh. Good. Well. Your first, uh, performance will be this Saturday, eight o'clock. My friends are throwing me a birthday party."

"Is that so?" He steered the car toward the entrance to Penn Station, looming ahead. To the tune of "Happy Birthday" he sang, "How old are you now?"

"How old do you think I am?"

A crack of laughter was his only answer. "I'm not naive enough to play that game with any woman. Come on—fess up."

"Thirty. I turned thirty last Saturday."

"Well, happy birthday. I'm five years past that myself. It wasn't so earth-shattering, the big three-oh."

It wouldn't be so earth-shattering for her, either, if not for a certain long-ago pact that had come back to haunt her.

The more she thought about it, the more she

realized that this was the ideal man to play the part of her significant other. Not only was he completely unknown to her friends, but there was no danger of him making more of it than there was. He was just a taxi driver, after all, doing a job to pick up extra cash—as if she'd hired him to mow her lawn or paint her house.

As soon as they pulled over at the curb, a trench-coat-clad man materialized, waiting with ill-disguised impatience for Amanda to relinquish the cab. She looked at the meter, opened her wallet and counted out the fare plus two hundred dollars. "Nikolaos, is it?"

"Only if you're my mom. Everyone else calls me Nick."

Leaning forward, she thrust the money at him. "The first installment on your fee, Nick."

He stared at the four fifties for a long moment, his eyes still concealed behind the sunglasses. This close, she took note of the faded jeans and threadbare T-shirt, the disheveled hair, the dark beard stubble that roughened his jaw.

What am I doing? she thought. Was she crazy to try to pass off this guy as her one and only? Raven, Sunny and Charli had only seen her on the arms of smooth-talking, upward-climbing, nattily attired gentlemen from her own elevated socioeconomic stratum. Nick Stephanos might be at the top of the cabbie food chain, but there was still a yawning evolutionary gap between him and the slicker-than-pond-scum types she normally kept company with.

Nick finally took the bills and pocketed them. "You're very trusting."

"Here's my card." She handed it over.

"Amanda Coppersmith," he read. "What do your meddling friends call you? Mandy?"

"Amanda." A reluctant smile pulled at her mouth. "Only my mom calls me Mandy."

Nick jotted his phone number on the back of her receipt, which Walt Frazier's recorded voice reminded her to take. "How far is the party from your place?" he asked, ignoring the man in the trench coat, now rapping on the window and glaring at her.

"About fifteen minutes."

"I'll pick you up Saturday at a quarter to eight."

"We'll take my car."

Nick handed her the receipt. "Call me old-fashioned, but as long as I'm the testosterone-based life-form, I'm driving." As if reading her mind, he added, "Don't worry, my personal vehicle doesn't have a meter. Now, go catch your train, boss. You're holding up my fare."

2

THEY'VE GOT TO BE KIDDING, Nick thought.

"They've got to be kidding," Amanda said.

They'd just stepped into the living room of the sprawling waterfront home owned by Amanda's friend Charli and her husband, Grant Sterling. After viewing the exterior of this impressive three-story house, with its granite-and-cedar construction and white Tuscan-style columns, he'd expected an equally elegant interior. And it was elegant.

If you didn't count the garish Happy Birthday banner and multicolored balloons, the bowls of Cheez Doodles and Goldfish crackers, and the Pin the Tail on the Donkey poster mounted on one wall.

And the clown. The clown done up in full regalia, down to the white-face makeup, bulbous red nose, Bozo hair and big floppy shoes. Not to mention the double bourbon on the rocks clutched in one white-gloved hand.

The party was already in full swing, with about thirty people enjoying cocktails and salty snacks, wearing pointy, glittery birthday hats and listening to a recording of *Sesame Street* songs.

Nick leaned close to Amanda and whispered, "You

said your friends were nosy busybodies. You didn't tell me they were demented."

"Oh, did I forget that part?" Amanda appeared shell-shocked.

Nick knew this wasn't her first eye-opener of the evening. That had come a short while earlier when he'd rung her doorbell. She'd failed to conceal her surprise—and relief—at his physical appearance. He wore a well-tailored sport coat and slacks, a collarless white twill shirt and polished loafers. He was freshly shaved, his hair neatly combed. "I clean up pretty good," he'd said when she stood mutely gaping at him. At least she'd had the grace to look embarrassed.

Last Monday when she'd let herself out of his cab, he'd watched her walk across the pavement and into the entrance to Penn Station. He'd watched her long legs, all the longer and more shapely for those spiked heels. He'd watched the delicious sway of her compact fanny under that short, snug skirt.

"I've had worse jobs," he'd told her. Understatement of the year.

Tonight she wore a short black cocktail dress, sheer black stockings and strappy high heels. Her only jewelry aside from diamond-and-black-pearl earrings was a brooch in the shape of a spider—eerily realistic, as if the diamond-encrusted bug were actually crawling up her shoulder.

Nick was beginning to detect a sartorial pattern: his new employer favored figure-hugging outfits short enough to show off those sensational legs. As for the spider pin, the nonverbal message seemed to be *If you don't get it, too darn bad.* It was the wardrobe of a woman comfortable with her body and confident of her own taste and appeal. Her pale, glossy hair swung free, just brushing her shoulders, in contrast to the tight, sophisticated do she'd worn for work.

As soon as her friends spotted the guest of honor, they swarmed her. Amid birthday wishes, kisses and hugs, Amanda managed to introduce her new "friend." Nick rattled off a string of polite greetings as he shook the hands of her meddlesome friends and their husbands.

"I'm so glad you could join us, Nick," Sunny said as she fitted him with a shiny red birthday hat, positioning it practically on his forehead like a unicorn horn and securing the short elastic string behind his head. Amanda rated a gold cardboard crown printed with the words *Birthday Girl* in pink and silver glitter.

She said, "I'm afraid to ask what inspired this particular theme."

"Don't you remember?" Raven said. "Last Sunday at Kirk and Sunny's wedding reception, when you told us not to throw you a party because you're not some little kid who needs—"

"Birthday candles and a pointy hat," Amanda finished in a tone that said she should have anticipated this bizarre result.

"We thought it sounded like a darn good idea," Charli said. "And lucky you—you got here just in time for musical chairs!"

An hour later, Nick and Amanda were ensconced on the short end of the L-shaped, beige suede sofa. He was sipping an India Pale Ale and playing with the tiny hand-held pinball game that was his prize for coming in first at duck, duck, goose.

Most of the other guests were clustered around the white fireplace mantel on the opposite side of the room, where Lucky the Clown, following his third double shot of Jack Daniel's, had begun entertaining the crowd by twisting long, skinny balloons into obscene shapes. "This is the besht goddamn party I've ever worked!" Lucky crowed.

Charli joined Sunny and Raven on the long end of the sofa. "So tell me." Charli leaned toward Nick. "How did the two of you meet?"

Nick slid his arm around Amanda's shoulders. "This beautiful lady just appeared in my taxi one day—" he felt her stiffen "—and we hit it off."

"What Nick means," Amanda quickly added, "is that, uh, we both went after the same taxi—I mean, we got into it at the same time and, uh, decided to share it."

"Oh yeah?" Raven smiled. "How romantic. When did this happen?"

Nick said "Monday" at the same instant that Amanda said "Wednesday."

Sunny laughed. "They're having disagreements already. Is that a good sign or a bad one?"

"We met on Wednesday," Nick said, and squeezed Amanda's shoulder. "It just feels like we've known each other a lot longer."

Raven said, "What do you do for a living, Nick?"

Obviously the truth wouldn't do; the boss lady had already made that clear. Before he had a chance to come up with an alternative career, Amanda jumped in with, "Nick owns a fleet of limos."

Her friends looked suitably impressed.

"But if you have all these limos at your disposal," Sunny asked him, "what were you doing taking a cab?"

If Amanda kept stiffening up like that, he thought, her muscles were going to cramp. "It's faster to hail a taxi than call for a limo," he casually drawled. "Besides, if I took one of my cars out of commission every time I needed a ride, it would wreck hell with the bottom line."

Kirk Larsen came up behind the sofa where Sunny sat. He placed his hands on his wife's shoulders, and she tipped her head back as he leaned down to kiss her. They made a striking couple. Several inches taller than Nick's own five-eleven, Kirk had blond hair practically to his shoulders, and pale blue eyes. Sunny's wavy, reddish-brown hair was quite long, the side strands secured with a pair of antique-looking barrettes. With her expressive violet eyes and vintage-style pastel dress, she looked like a winsome beauty from another era.

"Wish me luck," Kirk told the small group assembled on the sofa. "On Monday I go under the knife."

Everyone else seemed to know what he meant. Amanda turned to Nick and explained, "He's having his vasectomy reversed."

Nick experienced an instant and overwhelming urge to cross his legs. Clearly there was some history here of which he was unaware; Kirk must have been married before.

Amanda's younger brother, Jared, and his wife, Noelle, joined the group. The siblings shared a strong family resemblance, though Jared's coloring was slightly darker, his hair a deeper honey shade and his eyes more mossy-green than Amanda's silver-gray. Noelle had very short, very red hair and a well-padded physique that threatened to morph from pleasingly voluptuous to overly plump with her next doughnut.

Jared perched on the arm of the sofa next to his sister. "Wait till you see the birthday present Noelle and I got you."

Amanda adjusted her cardboard crown. "As long as it isn't a Barbie doll or Play-Doh, I'll be happy."

"That's all it takes?" Nick reached into the breast pocket of his sport coat and presented her with a tiny box wrapped in iridescent white paper and tied with gold ribbon. "Good to know."

Amanda stared wide-eyed at the dainty package. "What—what's this?"

Raven barely restrained a chuckle. "I believe it's called a birthday present."

"But...you didn't have to do this, Nick!"

"If you don't take it," Sunny warned her, "I will. Small means expensive. You like expensive."

At this, Amanda's expression became downright stricken. Now Nick was the one trying not to laugh. He asked, "Do I have to open it for you?"

Amanda made a conspicuous effort to compose herself. She accepted the gift with a weak smile and sent Nick a look that said this wasn't part of the bargain.

"Open it!" Noelle urged. "At this rate you'll never get through all your presents."

"This is..." Amanda said. "I mean, Nick and I have only known each other for five days."

"Three," Sunny said, "but who's counting?"

Amanda bit her lower lip. *That's right*, Nick silently reminded her. *You said we met Wednesday.* He had no sympathy. The woman should stick to the truth if she couldn't remember her fib from one moment to the next.

With obvious reluctance she pulled the ribbon off the present and plucked at the wrapping paper.

"Will you hurry up?" Sunny demanded.

"I think she's turning into my mother," Charli said with a smirk. "Mama folds wrapping paper and saves it—to reuse, she claims. 'What beautiful paper, such a shame to waste it.'"

"Meaning," Raven interpreted with a small smile, "what a shame to waste it on *her*, as if she's undeserving of such an honor. Tell me, has she ever reused any of it?"

"Never," Charli said. "She's got a ton of used wrapping paper stacked neatly in the attic. A real fire hazard. She always buys new—wouldn't be caught dead wrapping anyone else's birthday or Christmas gift in old paper!"

Amanda balled up the wrapping paper and hurled it at Charli. "Here. For Mama." She glanced at Nick and appeared to be holding her breath as she raised the hinged lid of the tiny mauve box she'd revealed. Her eyes went wide; her mouth parted. "It's...a whistle."

"A whistle?" Sunny craned her neck to see. Her eyes popped. "Wow! *What* a whistle!"

While Amanda's friends exclaimed over the gift, Amanda's gaze locked with Nick's. He could tell he'd surprised her. Again. He decided he liked doing that.

Jared lifted the small sterling silver bauble by its long, delicate chain and peered closely at it. The whistle had an old-fashioned shape, etched with curlicues and set with three semiprecious cabochon stones: green tourmaline, yellow citrine and purple amethyst. "Does it work?" he asked.

Nick said, "Try it."

He did. The result was a startlingly loud, shrill tone.

Noelle was next to inspect it, before handing it to Nick. "Can we assume this gift has some significance?"

"The first time I set eyes on Amanda," Nick said, as he fastened the chain around her neck, "she was hailing a taxi with a two-finger whistle that could've shattered glass."

Jared gave her a proud thump on the back. "That's my big sister!"

Amanda lifted the whistle off her dress to look at it closely. Her silver eyes flicked to Nick's, just for an instant, long enough to tell him the ride home would be interesting.

"Thank you, Nick." She pasted a polite smile on her face. "It's beautiful. And very unique."

Jared said, "He doesn't even get a kiss?"

"I think a present like that deserves a real toe-curling, tongue-tangling lip-lock myself," Sunny said, "but hey, that's just me."

Amanda gave Nick a quick peck on the cheek, obviously just to shut up her friends.

"She'll do better later, Nick," Kirk chuckled, "when there's no audience."

The guests who were congregated around Lucky the Clown let out a roar of salacious laughter. "If my ex-wife had ones like this," Lucky cried, wagging his latest balloon creation, "I'd still be married to her!"

Raven's husband, Hunter, detached himself from the crowd and joined the small group at the sofa. "That is one sick clown." He glanced around. "Amanda, I'm surprised your folks aren't here."

Nick had thought she'd been tense before, but that had been nothing compared to the sudden strain he now sensed, sitting so close to her. He turned to look at her; outwardly she appeared unchanged.

"Liv told me she was sorry but they couldn't make it," Raven said, presumably referring to Amanda's mother. "She didn't say why."

Amanda exchanged an unspoken communication with her brother, which Nick interpreted as *Let me handle this.*

"Mom and Dad are at a wedding," Amanda said, "the daughter of one of his business associates. They'd RSVP'd months ago and couldn't get out of it."

Sunny nodded in understanding. "We figured it had to be something important to keep them away."

Charli added, "I know they'd be here if they could."

3

"SO TELL ME, boss," Nick said, as he negotiated the long, meandering drive from Grant and Charli's house to the road. "Why'd you lie about when you and I met?"

He felt her gaze on him, in the dim interior of his three-year-old Subaru Forester. "On Monday, Raven and Sunny and Charli left my office with me," she said. "They saw me get into your cab, though I'm sure they took no notice of who was behind the wheel."

Of course not, he thought. He was just a taxi driver, after all. Who was more anonymous than a taxi driver?

"They saw me get in." Her voice was clipped. "And they saw the cab take off. With just me in it. My story, remember? About how we met? I said you grabbed the taxi at the same time I did. They'd know it couldn't have been Monday."

"Yeah, about that story." Nick stared through the windshield at the dark street, inadequately illuminated by streetlamps made to resemble quaint, old-fashioned gas lamps, complete with frosted glass and scrolled ironwork. Their hosts lived in one of the North Shore's most exclusive neighborhoods—a world away from the congested section of Astoria,

Queens, that he called home. "Why couldn't we have just stuck to the truth?" he asked. "That I drive a cab."

He knew the answer, of course, but it gave him a wicked sort of satisfaction to watch her squirm.

"Well, it's just..." Amanda chose her words with obvious care. "My friends are all familiar with the type of man I usually go out with." She seemed to think that was explanation enough.

"What type is that?" he asked.

"Um...professional men."

"Taxi driving is a profession."

"Yes. Of course. And a very honorable one." In the next instant she blurted, "Oh God, that sounded so condescending! You must think I'm the snottiest, most stuck-up bitch you've ever met."

He glanced at her just as they passed under one of those silly Victorian streetlamps, and saw nothing but sincerity. Still...

"I just need to know the rules of the game, boss," he said, "if I'm going to be convincing in the role of your lover."

She gave a little start at the word *lover*, and the physical relationship it implied.

"So what you're trying to say," he interpreted, "is that your meddlesome pals know you'd never be caught dead with a lowly taxi driver."

Her sigh was eloquent. "You seem determined to put the worst possible spin on this."

"But it's nothing more than the truth, isn't that so? You don't strike me as someone who shies away from telling it like it is."

"Are you enjoying this?" she muttered.

"Not especially, no. But hey, at least I own a fleet of limos."

"What was I supposed to tell them? That you're a neurosurgeon? A financial analyst? What if one of them asked you about it? It would look pretty suspicious if my new boyfriend couldn't converse intelligently about what he does for a living."

"You might be surprised what I can converse about—*intelligently*."

It took her a moment to respond. In a chastened tone of voice she said, "I suppose we should have discussed stuff like this beforehand."

"That might've been a good idea."

"Listen, Nick. Despite the way it looks, I'm not elitist. I just...I want this whole farce to be as convincing as possible. But somehow I've managed to insult you, and that was never my intention. Please accept my apology."

His fingers relaxed on the wheel. "Apology accepted, if you answer one more question."

"Okay," she said wearily, "let's have it."

"Why weren't your folks at the party?"

A thick silence was his only answer. He glanced at her. She stared straight ahead at the approaching headlights, her features set.

"Come on," he wheedled, "I won't tell your nosy buddies. I'm just curious."

"I explained it already."

"This important wedding they supposedly went to.

Right. What's this business associate's name? The one whose daughter is getting married tonight?"

"I will not be interrogated by you."

"Not by a mere hireling, you mean. Tell me, if I were a neurosurgeon, would you give me a straight answer?"

"Okay. I've got a question for *you*." She shifted in her seat to half face him. "Why did you buy me that expensive present?"

"It wasn't that expensive. It's silver, not gold or platinum." But with her obvious love of shopping and knowledge of jewelry, she no doubt realized the thing had cost about two hundred bucks—the equivalent of what she'd paid him so far for his services.

She said, "I can't accept it."

He laughed.

"I'm serious. I don't know what you thought you were doing, spending that kind of money on me—"

"Can't you just accept the thing gracefully?"

"It's not like it's a regular gift," she said. "It's not like we really know each other. Oh, why am I trying to explain this to you! You know exactly what I'm talking about. You're just trying to irritate me."

"And jeopardize a cushy job like this? Now, why would I do that?"

"I have no idea, but I'll tell you one thing. Any more stunts like that and this 'cushy job' is history. I'll find someone else to help get the Wedding Ring off my back."

"The what? The wedding ring?"

She clammed up, shifting back around to face forward once more.

"Is that code for something?" he asked.

Silence.

"Come on, boss, give it up. It's not like I'm someone who's really in your life. It's not like we really know each other," he said, parroting her words.

"Stop calling me boss."

"Why are you so determined to keep your friends from setting you up with some guy?"

"That's none of your business," she snapped.

"You don't want to get married again, is that it?"

After a brief pause, she asked, "How did you know I was married before?"

He said, "Grant mentioned it."

"I didn't hear him say anything."

"Were you monitoring all my conversations tonight?" She chose not to respond, and he asked, "Was it a bad divorce?"

"Try *two* bad divorces."

He gave a grunt of sympathy.

"Both within three years," she said. "The last one was final eleven months ago."

He whistled. "You don't fool around."

"I wish I did. If I'd just 'fooled around' instead of marrying the bastards, I could've saved myself a lot of pain."

"So that's what this is about. After two Mr. Wrongs, you've sworn off marriage forever."

"An oversimplification," she said tightly, "and I could do without the flip attitude."

"But that's it in a nutshell, right?"

"Did I mention this is none of your business?"

"Well, actually, it is my business. You've made it my business. Why would anyone believe you and I are an item if I don't even know the most basic things about you—like that fact that you've been divorced twice?"

She made an exasperated little sound, conceding the point, but not happy about it.

"Anything else I should know?" he asked. The only thing she'd shared with him on the ride to the party was what she did for a living.

"You should know I listen to classical music," she answered, "and that caffeine never touches my lips."

"Are you a natural blonde?"

"Yes. How long have you been a cabbie?" she shot back.

He grinned. "Six years. What's your favorite food?"

"Ethnicity or specific dish?"

"Ethnicity."

"Japanese."

That was what he would have guessed. "Specific dish."

She said, "My grandmother's steak-and-kidney pie."

"You're kidding."

"My turn. What kind of undies do you wear?" she asked. "Boxers or briefs?"

"Such a prosaic question," he drawled. "I'm disappointed in you."

"How come a New York City cabbie tosses out words like 'prosaic' in casual conversation?"

"I didn't realize it was such a stumper. You want me to tell you what it means?"

"I *know* what it means! Okay, let's get back to the undies. Boxers or briefs?"

"What makes you think I wear either?"

Amanda gave a snort of disbelief. "Briefs," she declared with authority. "Plain white ones, but you've been toying with the idea of trying those clingy boxer briefs that come in different colors."

"Is that the kind that spins your wheels?" Nick asked. "Or is it what you figure an overeducated cabbie would go for?"

"Have you ever been married?"

"Hey, that's your third question in a row. It's my turn."

"You aren't, are you?" Suddenly she sounded worried. "Married?"

"Why? What difference would that make?"

"Can't you just answer the question? It *would* make a difference."

"I don't see why. I'm just doing a job. Putting on a performance for your friends."

"I wouldn't want to...disrupt your personal life. Take you away from your wife on weekends. She might not understand that it's just, you know..."

"Business," he supplied, before putting her out of her misery. "I'm not married, Amanda. Never have been."

"Oh. Any particular reason?"

"I'll answer that if you tell me why you tied the knot with two losers who weren't right for you."

Predictably, that put an end to marriage-related talk. She pulled herself up straighter and reached behind her neck.

"You're going to return this for a refund," she told him, replacing the silver whistle in its little box.

"Yeah, right."

"Don't be stubborn."

"Your friends will expect to see you wearing it."

She chewed this over. "Then I'll reimburse you. How much was it?"

"What a rude question. I'm surprised at you."

"Don't make this difficult, Nick. I'll just guess at the amount and tack it onto your final payment."

"I won't take more than the fee we agreed upon. You tip cabbies, not actors."

"I refuse—"

"It's a *gift*, Amanda. Say thank you and enjoy the damn thing."

"I already said thank you," she muttered.

"You could say it like you mean it. A bit of a challenge for a control freak like you, but—"

"Control freak? Oh, please. Anytime a woman asserts herself, she's automatically a 'control freak.'"

He started to speak, but she cut him off. "The conversation is over," she snapped. "Just get me home. And in the future please keep in mind that ours is an employer-employee relationship. No more gifts. No more prying questions. Got that?"

"Got it. Boss."

Nick couldn't help but wonder how his "employer" would react if she knew the truth—that his participation in this charade had nothing to do with earning an easy grand.

4

IT'S A CONSPIRACY, Amanda thought with wry amusement, as she reached through the branches of a small tree, plucked a Winesap apple and dropped it into the bushel basket at her feet. Their fifth double date in two weeks! It seemed that every time she picked up the phone, it was either Charli or Raven or Sunny inviting her and Nick to do something as a foursome. And just last Tuesday, all four couples had spent an exhilarating evening at a Cajun restaurant with live zydeco music and a pecan-crusted catfish filet that was practically a religious experience.

For some reason, Amanda had never before gone apple-picking at any of the orchards open to the public, though it was an autumn tradition for many Long Islanders. It had taken yet another invitation, this one from Charli and Grant, to bring her and Nick out here to the North Fork for the day.

They'd stopped first at a pumpkin farm, where, at Hunter's request, the four of them had combed the sprawling field on a quest for several dozen various-sized pumpkins. These would be carved into jack-o'-lanterns to help decorate Stitches, the comedy club Hunter owned, where he and Raven planned to throw a spectacular private costume party for Halloween, only three days away.

"You know what's good, I see."

Amanda turned at the sound of Grant's voice. He set down his half-full basket and started pulling Winesaps off the same tree. The orchard was arranged in neat rows of small trees, each row bearing a sign identifying the variety of apple growing there. Beneath each tree lay a scattering of fruit that someone had judged imperfect. The afternoon was overcast; a chilly breeze bore the scents of the orchard to her nose: earth and cidery must and the green tang of the leaves.

She asked, "Where did my boyfriend and your wife wander off to?"

"Charli likes Golden Delicious, and she also wants to lay in some Cortlands for cooking. Nick is concentrating on McIntosh, I believe."

"They don't know how yummy these babies are," she said, picking another Winesap.

"More for us."

With his fortieth birthday a mere month away, Grant was nearly a decade older than his bride and her Wedding Ring friends. A high-powered matrimonial lawyer, he possessed a dignified bearing and a mature outlook on life, but he knew how to have fun, and he was the best thing that had ever happened to Charli. And he was a handsome devil, with thick, light brown hair and lively hazel eyes that crinkled at the corners when he smiled.

"Listen," Amanda said, "I hope that business about your friend James didn't cause any trouble for you."

Grant frowned. "James?"

"You know, your golfing buddy, the one Charli and the others tried to set me up with and I refused. And then I met Nick anyway, so..." She shrugged.

After a moment of cogitation he said, "Oh, you mean *Jimmy!* I always think of him as Jimmy, so when you said James..." He mimicked her shrug.

"I couldn't recall his last name," Amanda said. Either Grant's reaction was a little fishy or Amanda was letting her suspicious nature get the better of her. "What is it again?"

"What?"

"Jimmy's last name."

"Oh, uh..." His gaze landed beyond Amanda's shoulder, and she realized why when she heard Charli answer for him.

"Selden," Charli said, as she came up behind Amanda. "James Selden."

"I always look forward to golfing with Jimmy." Grant tossed another two apples into his basket. "His swing's so bad, he makes even me look good by comparison."

"So anyway," Amanda said, "I hope it wasn't too awkward for you guys, having to rescind Jimmy's invitation to my birthday party."

"Don't worry about it." Grant winked. "He met a Norwegian architect named Olga."

"So it all worked out," Charli said.

"That's great." Amanda cocked her head. "An architect, huh? What does Jimmy do for a living?"

Charli and Grant said, "He's a—" at the same time.

With a little chuckle, Grant deferred to his wife, who answered, "He's a real estate developer." A fact Amanda already knew, from that conversation two and a half weeks ago when her Wedding Ring pals ambushed her at the office. Either this James Selden did indeed exist and was indeed a real estate developer, or Charli had also remembered the career Raven had mentioned.

Or it could be that I'm paranoid and delusional, seeing conspiracies and flimflams where none exist.

After all, why would her friends invent a nonexistent man for her to meet? How would that possibly fit into any matchmaking scheme?

It didn't, Amanda decided. They just wanted her to be happy. They were misguided but sincere. Why couldn't she just accept that?

Because she'd known these gals for a quarter of a century, that was why. The ill-fated introduction to this Jimmy guy might've been on the up and up, but the Wedding Ring had *some* underhanded plot perking away; she'd bet her best Prada handbag on it.

Amanda jumped when a long, masculine arm snaked around her from behind, then she gave a self-conscious little laugh. She didn't have to look to know who it was; she recognized Nick's pleasant, subtle scent.

Not for the first time, she felt a little thrill of pride at her man's good looks and raw sex appeal, and immediately squelched the foolish thought. That kind of pride had no place in this business arrangement. The only thing she should feel proud about was that she'd concocted such an effective plan and had had the confidence and nerve to put it into action.

But how relieved she'd been the night of her birthday party when a scrubbed-shiny Nick had rung her doorbell! She'd fretted for five days, certain that the guest of honor would be making her appearance on the arm of Travis Bickle, Robert De Niro's scruffy title character from the movie *Taxi Driver*.

As it turned out, De Niro at his best had nothing on Nick Stephanos. Nick's athletic physique looked just as scrumptious in a tailored suit as it did in snug jeans and a T-shirt. His eyes, once she'd gotten a good look at them, were a warm shade of brown that varied with his moods from amber to molasses.

His hair was thick and short and black as jet, like the glossy pelt of some exotic animal. If he were her boyfriend for real, she'd give in to her curiosity and touch it. As it was, she settled for imagining how it would feel sliding between her fingers. Was the texture silky or coarse?

She leaned back against Nick as he loosely wrapped his arms around her, just under her breasts. He'd gradually been doing that more and more, cozying up to her the way a real boyfriend might. With all these double and quadruple dates they'd been on recently, she and Nick had had ample opportunity to convince her pals that theirs was a bona fide romantic relationship. And they must have been doing something right—her friends had yet to challenge her sincerity.

Nick's current demonstration proved just as credi-

ble. Grant and Charli seemed to accept without question the affectionate way Nick held her, the casual kiss
he placed on her temple. His warm breath teased her
ear, sending a shiver skating up her spine.

This part of their playacting, the physical part, had
turned out to be much less onerous than Amanda had
anticipated. Perhaps it was because Nick was so relaxed about it. The guy was one hell of an actor.

Either that or he found the experience as pleasur-
able as she did.

Amanda couldn't lie to herself. She liked it. She
liked it whenever she and Nick were sitting together
and he'd slide his arm around her shoulders and pull
her a little closer—a seemingly automatic gesture, devoid of subterfuge.

She liked it whenever they were dining in a restaurant and he'd bring his fork to her lips so she could
sample what he'd ordered, his eyes molten onyx by
candlelight, his megawatt smile drawing her like a
lighthouse beacon.

She even liked it on those rare occasions when he
bestowed a light kiss on her lips.

All for the sake of their watchful audience, of
course. Whenever her friends left and she found herself alone with her "boyfriend," he turned into the
consummate gentleman, keeping his hands and his
lips and his hot, seductive eyes to himself.

The rational side of Amanda knew why she found
pleasure in Nick's caresses, even though theirs was a
fictitious relationship, even though they didn't really

know each other and she'd never have chosen to go out with him under normal circumstances.

It was *because* she'd never have gone out with him. Nick wasn't her type, and anyway, he was only after a quick buck. With him, there was no danger of anything serious developing, no danger of the dreaded Commitment rearing its ugly head, no danger of her horrific personal history repeating itself. Not with this man, not with the "hired help." Thus she was free to simply relax and enjoy the physical sensations for what they were, the snuggling and the kisses and the flirtatious glances she shared with him when her eagle-eyed buddies were hovering nearby.

After all, it wasn't as if she were going to hop into bed with the man. What harm was there in enjoying a counterfeit cuddle or two?

Amanda twisted a little in Nick's arms to look at him. She should have expected his response: a warm smile and an even warmer kiss. Maybe a part of her *had* expected it; maybe that was why she'd done it.

Maybe she should throttle back the physical stuff before she got to like it *too* much.

Amanda eased herself out of his embrace. "Did you only get McIntosh?"

"Some Macs, some Red Delicious..." Nick had been stowing his harvest in a plastic grocery bag. He now upended the bag into Amanda's bushel basket, filling it to the brim.

"Don't do that!" she cried, watching his apples mingle with hers. "How will we ever get them separated?"

"Why separate them?" Nick waved away her concern. "We'll just keep them at your place. You've got more space for them anyway, your fridge is empty—if you don't count that lone carton of yogurt that's applied for permanent residence."

She made a face at him as Charli rose to her defense. Sort of. "Hey, that's not fair. She's also got a bottle of Pellegrino water in there."

"Okay," he said. "One itty-bitty container of fat-free, sugar-free yogurt and some fancy bottled water. I think we can find room for—" he gave the basket an experimental tug "—eighty pounds or so of apples."

Nick's casual reference to sharing her refrigerator sent a jab of apprehension through Amanda, prompting her sensible side to kick in.

It's all part of the act, she assured herself. He wasn't really encroaching on her space. He wasn't really going to be in her house every day eating these apples and leaving his razor in her bathroom and taking up all kinds of psychic space. *He wasn't really her boyfriend, for crying out loud!*

"Are these good?" Nick plucked a Winesap off the tree and chomped into it. "Not bad. Not a Mac, but it's got appeal."

He left the lousy pun hanging there, not deigning to acknowledge his companions' good-natured groans as he quickly reduced the apple to a scraggly core and picked three more off the tree.

Amanda said, "You know, you're supposed to pay for those things before you eat them."

"We're buying a hundred pounds—"

"Oh, so now it's a *hundred* pounds."

"—and I figure they can spare a free taste. Did you know I'm a man of many talents?" Nick started juggling the apples like a pro. It was really quite impressive.

"Hey," Grant said, "you could've provided entertainment at Amanda's birthday party."

"And compete with Lucky the Potty-Mouthed Clown? I'll stick to amazing my nieces and nephews until they get too worldly and sophisticated, and lock embarrassing old Uncle Nick in the cellar when their friends come over."

Amanda flashed on an image of Nick juggling for a gaggle of children. She hadn't given much thought to his personal life, other than to ascertain that there was no Mrs. Stephanos to wreak havoc with her plans. She hadn't pictured him as a member of a family, with brothers and sisters and nieces and nephews.

She knew he drove in from the city whenever he picked her up, but she had no idea where exactly he lived, whether in Manhattan or one of the outlying boroughs. She couldn't imagine he had the income to live in Manhattan, but if he'd been fortunate enough to snag a rent-controlled apartment, then she supposed it was possible.

It embarrassed her now that she'd never bothered to ask Nick something so basic as where he lived. She'd never asked him anything about himself, for that matter, never expressed interest in him as a person, after that night when he'd driven her home from her birthday party and they'd played at interrogating

each other. But that had been only a game, one she'd
lost control of all too quickly.

There it was again. Control. He'd called her a control freak. She'd denied it, of course. But Amanda
wasn't very good at believing her own lies. If she
were, perhaps she'd be a happier person.

She was wearing the silver whistle Nick had given
her. His arm bumped it where it rested just under the
curve of her breasts over her taupe cashmere sweater.
He lifted the whistle and absentmindedly toyed with
it, rubbing it between his fingers, peering into it. As he
did so, his flannel-clad forearm grazed her breasts,
just slightly, sending tiny electric jolts through her.

"Do you use this?" Nick asked. "To hail taxis?"

"When I'm wearing it."

She felt his eyes on the side of her face, as if gauging
her veracity. He asked, "Really?"

"Well...I usually forget I have it. Habits of a lifetime
are hard to break."

His chuckle warmed her cheek, and she tried to
imagine the picture her words conjured in his head.
An elegantly attired New York businesswoman flag-
ging down a cab with a two-finger whistle that, as
he'd so aptly noted, could shatter glass—while a
dainty yet perfectly functional whistle hung around
her neck. Amanda smiled.

Grant said, "Maybe you should've given her a meg-
aphone."

Nick let the whistle drop. "There's always next
year."

Well, no, there wasn't. January 11 would mark the

three-month point in their "relationship." As long as she and Nick had become legitimately engaged in the eyes of her Wedding Ring pals by January 11, she could call it quits and be officially immune from further matchmaking efforts.

Raven and Sunny had both tried to weasel out of the Wedding Ring pact, and failed, because they'd waited until they were already seriously involved with the chosen man and things had begun to get complicated. Even Charli had finally given up on her coldly practical marriage of convenience to Grant, with more than a month to go on her three-month "obligation" to the Wedding Ring.

Of the four of them, only Amanda was a successful entrepreneur in the true sense, the CEO of a corporation with a payroll, 401K and dental plans, and dressdown Fridays. Thus only Amanda possessed the acumen and foresight that had allowed her to predict the unhappy tangle her life could become if her wellmeaning friends had their way. Not to mention the superior negotiating skills that had allowed her to nip the Wedding Ring pact in the bud.

Come January 11, she'd be a free woman. If Nick's mention of next year's birthday present made her a tad wistful, she blamed her sentimental friends and their insistence that they knew better than she what she needed to make her happy.

Grant turned to his wife. "Are you ready?"

"I think so." Charli lifted her bulging grocery bag. "I'll be busy for weeks trying out new recipes."

"We'll meet up with you by the car," Grant called

over his shoulder as he and Charli started down the row of trees.

Nick said, "I take it Charli likes to cook."

"Oh, she's a fabulous cook. You should taste her spinach-stuffed ravioli. She puts me to shame."

He was watching her closely. "That isn't just an expression for you, is it? You really feel that way—that she puts you to shame."

"Well, when it comes to cooking." Amanda picked an apple and turned it in her hand, admiring the shape of it and the dark red skin. "I've honestly tried to learn. I even took a class to learn how to construct sushi. Figured at least that was something I couldn't burn."

"Ah yes, you did say you like Japanese food. Did you get any good at it?"

Amanda shook her head. "My maki rolls fall apart. And my other efforts resemble chum on a bed of sticky rice. The class was a waste of time and money."

"Did you enjoy it?"

"What?"

"Taking the class. Watching the teacher. Schmoozing with the other students. Eating the samples. Did you enjoy it?" he repeated.

"Well, yeah, I guess so."

"Then it wasn't a waste. And as for being a failure as a sushi chef—"

Something inside Amanda flinched at the word *failure*.

"—just remember, there's no shame in trying and

failing. If you were too wimpy to even try, now, that would be something to be ashamed of."

"No one's ever accused me of being wimpy. Mouthy, opinionated and bitchy on occasion, but never wimpy."

"Bitchy? You?"

He gave her a charmingly dubious smile, and Amanda wondered whether he seriously couldn't picture her as a bitch or he had no problem doing so and was simply being sarcastic. For some reason, it mattered.

"That's another of those words used to keep women in their place," she said.

"I've heard how that one goes. When a man takes charge, everyone admires his assertiveness. When a woman does the same thing, she's called a bitch."

"You don't think that double standard really exists, do you?" Prickles of angry heat stung Amanda's face. "Or maybe you know damn well it does and you think that's just fine—the natural order and all that."

He laughed. "Not that you're trying to put words in my mouth. What did I ever say or do to come off looking like a troglodyte?"

Another ten-dollar word. No, Amanda mused, she really didn't know all that much about Nikolaos Stephanos.

She said, "This from the man who insisted that driving was the prerogative of testosterone-based life-forms."

"Anyone ever tell you you don't know how to take a joke?"

"You were joking when you said that? So you won't mind if I drive us back."

Nick gave a be-my-guest shrug, fished his car keys out of his pocket and held them out to her.

Amanda reached for the keys. Her hand stalled in midair. There hadn't been any space left in the orchard's parking lot when they'd arrived, and excess vehicles were parked haphazardly on the shoulder of the gravel road. Nick, with his prodigious skill, had barely managed to wedge his white Forester between a couple of Harleys and a camper, their bumpers practically kissing. She'd never get his car out of that automotive jigsaw puzzle without sacrificing some paint at the very least.

"I'm...not used to driving an SUV," she said.

"There's nothing to it." He jangled the keys. "It's just like a regular car."

"Well, I really don't know. I'm not...it's not that I..."

He returned the keys to his pocket, with a knowing smile that made those prickles burn hotter.

Damn it, she *never* blushed!

"Next time," she said tightly, "we'll take my car."

"You got it, boss."

"Don't call me—"

"If we don't get a move on, Charli and Grant will think we decided to camp out here."

He easily lifted the overburdened bushel basket. His biceps inflated, straining the seams of his flannel sleeves; the cords stood out in his wrists. Those flimsy wire handles had to be digging into his fingers, but he never uttered a complaint as he led the way to the counter where the fruit was weighed and paid for, and down the road toward the car. She insisted she could carry some of the apples in bags or in another basket, but all he said was, "Why? It's not that heavy."

"Nick, I was wondering. Where do you live?"

"Queens."

"Oh." The city's largest borough. "Where in Queens?"

"Astoria."

"Astoria! I know Astoria."

He glanced at her. "You've been there?"

"Well, no. I mean, I know something about it. Weren't the old movies made there?"

He nodded. "It was the original Hollywood. There's still a big studio complex in Astoria. A bunch of movies and TV shows are made there."

"Huh. I didn't know that."

"Then I'll tell you something else you didn't know. There's a strong Greek presence in Astoria."

"And a strong Greek present here," Amanda teased, touching his upper arm as they walked side by side. It was as solid as a tree trunk.

He smiled; the dimple winked. She had to look away. Sometimes this man was just too damn appealing. She found it was getting harder and harder to keep the point of all this in perspective.

And she had to keep it in perspective. Otherwise...

She *had* to keep it in perspective! "Otherwise" was not an option!

She spotted Nick's white Forester. Getting it out of there would be an even greater challenge than before, courtesy of a double-parked silver Miata. Grant and Charli, leaning on the hood and munching apples, waved to them.

"Tell me something," Nick asked. "Why couldn't you have just admitted you don't trust your driving skills enough to get my car out of that tangle?"

She could have denied it, and made herself look even more foolish. Amanda wasn't used to feeling foolish. She found she didn't like it.

When she remained mute, he said, "You don't have to be good at everything, Amanda."

The quiet understanding in his tone slammed through her defenses like a battering ram. She blinked against the sudden burning behind her eyelids.

She felt his gaze on her, fleetingly. Just before they reached the Forester he muttered, "I never could stomach sushi, anyway."

A watery snort of laughter erupted from her.

"Ah, ever the lady."

Grinning, she wiped her eyes. "Shut up and drive."

5

HE LIVES OVER A BAR.

Amanda stood on the sidewalk of a busy block in Astoria, Queens, craning her neck to stare up at the plain little second-story windows above Benny's Clubhouse Tavern. It was close to 8:00 p.m., the sky fully dark. Light shone between the slats of the closed wooden blinds. He was home.

Her gaze slid down the building's redbrick facade. The names of featured beers glowed neon-bright in the windows of the tavern, and a large sign advertised Live Music Every Monday, Wednesday And Saturday! Another sign informed her that a band called Bad Habit would be playing tonight and Wednesday, followed by Little Sammy and the Underachievers on Saturday.

A trio of young men threw open the door on their way inside, letting out a gust of warm air that reeked of fried food and tobacco smoke and stale beer. She heard raucous conversation and the crack of billiard balls colliding.

Amanda located the door to the upstairs apartments between the tavern and the party supply store next to it. She double-checked the gold-and-black stick-on address numbers to verify this was indeed home sweet home. It was. She'd looked him up in the Astoria phone directory.

Two dented steel mailboxes, belonging to Apartments 1 and 2, were bolted to the brickwork inside the doorway overhang, as was an intercom with two buttons. Amanda peered at the little labels identifying the tenants. Someone named C. O'Leary lived in Apartment 1. Apartment 2 belonged to N. Stephanos.

The pair of zippered plastic garment bags hanging over her right arm grew progressively heavier as she stood there wondering whether to push the button or hightail it back to her brand-new hunter-green Jaguar XKR, parked around the corner. Finally she hefted the bags to her left arm, which caused the slim chain-and-leather strap of her Chanel purse to slide off the shoulder of her sky-blue wool crepe suit jacket. She yanked it back up and pressed the intercom button. And waited.

Nothing happened. Amanda stabbed the button three times in rapid succession. She was about to lean on the thing when Nick abruptly demanded, "Who is it?" She'd never heard him sound so gruff. It took her a few moments to realize that his voice hadn't issued from the intercom.

"I said who's out there?" he barked.

Amanda stepped back from the doorway and blinked up at the second-floor windows, one of which had been thrown open.

"Amanda?" Nick leaned out of the building. His hair appeared disheveled. He was shirtless. "I wasn't expecting you."

"I...I should've called. I can come back some other—"

"No problem. Come on up, boss."

"Don't call me— Oh, the hell with it," she muttered. He'd already disappeared. Moments later the nerve-grating door buzzer sounded. Shifting the garment bags again, she grabbed the door handle and let herself into the cramped stair landing, spookily lit by an old-fashioned milk-glass ceiling fixture.

Nick appeared at the top of the stairs, near the open door to Apartment 2. He was still bare above the waist, his jeans zipped but the brass button unfastened, as if he'd hurriedly stepped into them. He was barefoot.

"Intercom's on the fritz. Here, let me help you with that." He met her halfway up the stairs. Gratefully she relinquished the bags. "I can guess what these are," he said.

"And I'm sure you'd guess right." Hunter and Raven's Halloween party was tomorrow night. After work, Amanda had gone to a party rental place near her home to pick up the costumes she and Nick would wear.

"Didn't we agree that I'd swing by your office tomorrow to get my costume?" He preceded her up the stairs and held the door to his apartment open. "You didn't have to make a special trip."

Amanda hesitated on the threshold. Music drifted from the apartment, an intriguing, high-energy violin piece that toed the line between Latin and Celtic. "Well, I figured it was a nice night for a drive, so what the heck." That was her prepared excuse. In truth, she was more curious than she had a right to be about where her phony-baloney boyfriend hung his hat.

She knew she hadn't fooled him for an instant when he said, "Well, now that you're here..." and jerked his head toward the doorway.

"I—I really shouldn't. I didn't intend to disrupt your evening, I just figured I'd give you the costume and, you know..." Amanda shuffled back from the doorway.

"Then why did you haul both of them up here?"

"What?"

He indicated the bags he held. "Mine and yours."

"Oh, I just thought you might like to see mine. The two of them together. You know, before tomorrow night." She tugged ineffectually at the bag that she knew held her costume. "But it's really not that—"

"Come on in, then. Let's take a look at them."

Nick took hold of her elbow and propelled her inside the apartment. Then Amanda could only stare in wonder at her surroundings. Whatever she'd expected of an over-the-tavern blue-collar bachelor pad, this wasn't it. The furnishings were eclectic, understated pieces in warm neutral tones. An unusual Asian rug of bold geometric patterns partially covered the pale, pickled-oak floorboards.

She saw a futon sofa, a coffee table of distressed steel and glass, a pair of leather butterfly chairs and an exquisitely crafted long, low cabinet of some sort of reddish-toned burled wood. All the furnishings were low to the floor, giving the impression of an inviting space where comfort and relaxation reigned.

The walls were pure white. A double row of framed black-and-white photographs hung at eye level over the cabinet. The pictures featured such diverse subjects as a Lower East Side pickle merchant proudly displaying his wares, a straight-on view of New York City's Flatiron Building, a trio of children climbing an enormous boulder in Central Park, and a kilt-wearing street musician playing bagpipes on a Manhattan corner.

A rough-textured tapestry, obviously hand-woven, took up most of the opposite wall. Angular images of wolves and birds were repeated in a primitive design that had a distinctly South American look.

The lighting was low and warm and welcoming. Amanda had assumed that the apartment would be pervaded by smells and noise from below, but all she heard was the violin music coming from the stereo speakers. And the only odor her nose detected was the soapy, steamy scent of a recent shower. Nick's short, black hair spiked every which way, as if he'd just toweled it.

Nick laid the garment bags on the sofa and turned up the nearby floor lamp for extra light. He unzipped the top bag and pulled out a clothes hanger draped in froths of sheer teal-colored material shot through with gold threads. Beneath it hung a long, slinky dress of a paler teal with gold trim. There was also a bag of accessories, including such seductress essentials as a gold circlet-type headdress and several wide brace-lets.

Amanda watched him examine the outfit. He rubbed the filmy fabric between his fingers and held the dress up to the light. It was low-cut and sleeveless. And it looked even smaller and flimsier in his big hands.

Suddenly she wished they'd gone with her first choice, Bonnie and Clyde. But Nick had objected to dressing like a 1930s gangster. The costume would be too hot in a crowded party setting, he'd insisted, and besides, what was so special about a pin-striped suit and fedora?

"Fine," she'd said, "if you don't want to be overburdened with clothing, let's go as Tarzan and Jane." A loincloth—nice and cool. They'd compromised on Samson and Delilah.

Nick held her costume up to her. He wore an impish grin. "You going to model it for me?"

She snatched it out of his grasp and stuffed it back in the bag. "You'll have to wait till tomorrow. Let's check yours out."

The first thing Nick pulled out of the other bag was a long wig of wavy brown hair twisted into ropelike strands and tied back with a leather thong. "I told you." He tossed it on the sofa. "No wig."

"Just try it on." Amanda picked up the wig and tried to place it on his head, but he was having none of it. "It's not at all feminine looking," she said. "It's very butch—I mean, Samson's strength was his hair, right? Just give it a try. Please?"

"This isn't a macho issue for me. It's about comfort. I'm not going to go the whole night with that heavy, itchy thing on my head."

"But you're *Samson!*" She shook the wig in his face. "How can you be Samson without hair?"

"I have hair." He smoothed down his own damp strands and gave her a canny look. "I have about as much as Delilah left him with."

Amanda mulled it over. "You want to be Samson after she's lopped off his hair? Who's going to get that?"

"Everyone will get it if you wear a big pair of scissors on your belt."

"She used a knife. They didn't have scissors back then."

"Creative license—our Delilah had scissors. How about this? I'll find you a big, showy pair of scissors between now and tomorrow night."

"A blunt, fake pair. I don't want to end up sliced and diced."

"I'll find them somewhere."

"But if you're Samson after his haircut, you'd be in chains." She smiled. "And an itty-bitty loincloth."

"Loincloth, huh? Now we're back to Tarzan."

"You know what I mean. I don't know what it's called. One of those little slave getups that just cover the bare essentials. Don't you go to the movies?"

"You're really itching to see me in a loincloth, aren't you?"

Amanda didn't dare tackle that one. Even now, she was making a heroic effort to keep her gaze directed at

Nick's face rather than the delicious expanse of muscular male flesh on display between his chin and his waist.

"And another thing," she said. "If Delilah's already done her dirty work, you'd have to be blind. They put out Samson's eyes once his strength was gone. Haven't you read the Bible? Or seen the miniseries? So you might want to rethink the wig."

"Blind?" he said. "Cool. I'll wear my shades."

"A biblical character in sunglasses? Nick, come on—work with me here!"

"I'll find some wrist shackles between now and then," he said. "See? I'm working with you."

Amanda lifted Nick's costume out of the bag: a short-sleeved, belted tunic of dark red cloth, suitably biblical looking, especially when paired with the short togalike robe of a slightly darker hue that draped one shoulder. She rummaged in the bottom of the garment bag and located Samson's accessories, including leather sandals and a headband.

"Looks like we're set," he said. "I'll pick you up at eight?"

Before she could answer, a female voice called out from the back of the apartment, "Nicky?"

Amanda's heart jumped into her throat. Her first thought was *He's cheating on me!* In the next instant, reason prevailed and she realized with dismay that she'd interrupted some intimate scene.

But it sure felt like he was cheating on her.

As Amanda verbally stumbled over an attempt to get the hell out of there, her face flaming—damn it, she never never *never* blushed!—Nick nonchalantly gestured for her to stay put and disappeared into what she could only assume was his bedroom.

Amanda stood there feeling like a world-class fool and listening to the muted sounds of conversation. She couldn't make out what Nick was saying to his lady friend. Probably something along the lines of *Believe me, baby, it's just business! Give me a minute and I'll get rid of her.*

She could only wonder why he'd even let her into the apartment.

The answer came like a punch to the solar plexus. *Because it's just business. Because you have no place in his personal life, so what does it matter if you drop by while he's entertaining a girlfriend?*

Amanda cleared her throat. She called out, "Nick? I'm, uh, just gonna get going now."

"Wait a sec!" More unintelligible conversation, followed by the trill of feminine laughter.

Amanda zipped her garment bag so fast a bit of teal fabric got caught in the teeth. She pulled hard on the zipper tab and yanked ferociously at the delicate material.

"Whoa." Nick's hands took over the task. She hadn't heard him come up behind her. He'd donned a gray T-shirt and running shoes, she noticed. "You're gonna end up shredding this outfit—and there's not that much there to begin with. Damn," he muttered when his gentler efforts proved fruitless. He looked past Amanda and asked, "Are you any good with this sort of thing, Mrs. K.?"

Amanda followed his gaze and found herself staring at a tiny, ancient woman with a cap of snow-white curls.

Nick made the introductions. "Amanda Coppersmith, Mrs. Konstantopoulos, my landlady."

Amanda felt dizzy with relief. She told herself it was relief at being spared the ordeal of an Awkward Situation, and nothing more.

Unfortunately, she still wasn't very good at believing her own lies. She'd have to work on that.

"It's very nice to meet you, Mrs. Konstantopoulos." Amanda held out her hand.

Nick's landlady took it, clearly surprised and pleased at hearing her name pronounced correctly by someone she'd just met. Her seamed face spread in a wide grin. Putting names to faces, and getting those names right, was a skill Amanda had cultivated for business reasons. Nothing was so sweet to a person as the sound of his or her own name. The old woman's hand was gnarled and bony, the knuckles misshapen. Amanda shook it very gently.

As Nick and his landlady continued their lively conversation, in Greek, Mrs. K. shooed his hands away from the garment bag and applied her arthritic fingers to the chore. It took her about three seconds to free the fabric from the zipper.

Facing Nick, she gave him a fierce scowl. "*E'na mi'nas*," she said, holding up one finger.

Nick's expression was pleasant as he shook his head and countered with two fingers. "*Di'o.*"

Amanda didn't need anyone to tell her there was some serious negotiating going on.

Nick gesticulated toward his bedroom as he made his case, whatever it was. Listening to him speak a foreign tongue made him seem even more exotic and removed from Amanda's world—and, she was forced to admit, more fascinating than ever.

Which, all things considered, was not a good thing.

Amanda could tell that Nick had won the argument when Mrs. K. flapped her hand at him and grumbled, *"Ne, di'o, di'o."* She buttoned her plaid wool coat over her flowered housedress, then extracted a small object from her handbag and painstakingly unfolded the accordion pleats to reveal one of those clear plastic rain bonnets Amanda thought they'd stopped making around 1965.

"Mrs. Konstantopoulos," Amanda said, "it's not raining. I was just outside." Not a cloud in the night sky.

As the old woman snapped the bonnet under her chin and picked up her long, black umbrella, Nick sent Amanda a look that told her not to bother with reason. Clearly Mrs. K. was set in her ways. She bade Amanda *"Andi'o,"* before shuffling out the door on Nick's arm.

He signaled Amanda that he'd be back in a minute, then escorted his landlady down the stairs. Amanda crossed to the street-side window and watched the two emerge from the building, watched Nick help Mrs. K. into the driver's seat of a parked Taurus. Then he stood on the sidewalk and flinched as the old woman tore out into traffic amid the squeal of tires and honking of horns.

When he returned, Nick said, "I've been trying to get that woman to give up her driver's license for I don't know how long. She's a menace on the road."

"How old is she?"

"She admits to eighty-nine. Add a decade."

Amanda smiled. "She seems like a real character, but a sweet old lady underneath it all."

"That 'sweet old lady' has some unfortunate habits—such as letting herself in here with her master key, without warning. Tonight she only rousted me out of the shower. Her timing's been worse on occasion."

Amanda's imagination filled in the blanks. She pictured this virile man burning up the sheets with some girlfriend, only to have his elderly landlady barge in on them. When Amanda realized the girlfriend in this imaginary scenario looked just like her, she jettisoned the image from her mind. "What were you two haggling over?" she asked.

"I did some carpentry work in the bedroom, at her request. Built-in bookshelves. I asked for two months free rent in exchange. She only wanted to give me one. It's worth three months easy, but Mrs. K. thinks bread still costs a quarter." His shrug said *What are you gonna do?*

"So you're handy with a hammer and nails."

"Didn't I tell you I'm a man of many talents?"

"Do those talents extend to photography?" Amanda indicated the row of framed photos.

Nick nodded. "Sometimes I'll spend my whole day off just wandering around the city snapping pictures. Nothing's more relaxing."

She stood in front of a picture that appeared to have been taken in Harlem. Two girls twirled a pair of ropes while a third did some fancy double Dutch jumping. The photo captured the sense of movement and the girls' raw exhilaration.

"These are excellent," Amanda said, and meant it. "Have you ever sold your photos?"

"Then it wouldn't be relaxing, it'd be work." He came to stand next to her; Amanda felt the heat radiating from him. "No," he said, "this is just for me."

He was too close. She couldn't think when he was this close. The music stopped and she took the opportunity to step away from him. Strolling to the stereo in the corner, she said, "I've never heard violin playing like that. Who is it?"

"Eileen Ivers. Do I make you nervous?"

"No. Of course not." She flashed him a small smile to bolster the lie.

His eyes saw too much. Amanda's gaze scampered away. She looked around the living room. "I have to admit, this place isn't what I expected. You know. From the outside."

"Can I get you something to drink? I'm fresh out of jasmine tea...."

She smirked. While Nick had learned early on that jasmine tea was her hot beverage of choice, she doubted he'd ever brought any into his home. He favored black, caffeine-laden coffee, the stronger the better.

"No Pellegrino either," he continued. "I've got beer and orange juice. Oh, and a couple of cans of ginger ale. Not diet, though."

"Thanks, but I really can't stay. I just wanted to—"

"To bring the costume by. I know." He leaned against the low cabinet and crossed his arms. "So what *were* you expecting when you came up here? Peeling paint on cinder-block walls? Furniture I beat the garbagemen to? Pizza boxes stacked up? A pyramid of empty beer cans in the corner?"

Amanda took a deep breath, torn between diplomacy and honesty. One look at Nick's perceptive eyes, now the color of bittersweet chocolate, settled it.

"Something like that," she admitted. She spread her arms. "Nick, this place is really nice. You've obviously gone to some trouble to make it that way. How can you stand to live over a *bar?*"

"What's wrong with living over a bar?"

"Oh, come on." Now that the stereo was no longer on, she heard the low rumble of activity from below. "What happens when that rock band starts up?"

"Usually I listen for a while, and if I like the music, I go downstairs for a drink."

She tossed up her hand. "There. See? You can't even have quiet on a Monday, Wednesday or Saturday night."

"I'm not a big one for absolute silence. And anyway, the tunes from downstairs are never that loud up here. I always have the stereo or TV on anyway, and that drowns it out."

"The smells, then."

"What smells?"

"Don't tell me the cooking smells from that bar never come in here."

"Sure they do, a little, when I have the windows open. So what? It's a good smell. I eat a lot of my meals down there. Benny makes the best burgers around—ten ounces of prime sirloin on a big, crusty roll with nacho cheese and a pile of grilled onions. And their thick-cut fries! Now I'm getting hungry. Wanna go down for a bite?"

"You're impossible."

"Why? Because I like where I live? Amanda, you're out of touch. Over-the-store apartments have become a very desirable commodity."

"Oh, please."

"It's true. The whole social status of it has changed. Young people, singles and couples, are begging for places like this. Nowadays if you want one in this area, you have to get on a waiting list. Especially for a two-bedroom like this."

Amanda eyebrows lifted. "You have two bedrooms?"

Nick nodded. "The second one's my carpentry workroom. It's a very sociable way to live. I know all my neighbors and the shop owners around here and they know me—at the bakery, the produce stand, the coffee shop, everywhere."

Amanda had to admit the small-town environment

he described sounded appealing. The irony was that Nick lived in New York City, while she owned a lovely private home in a fashionable area of Long Island—a true small town. Yet she couldn't say when she'd last spoken to her own next-door neighbors, aside from hurried greetings in passing.

"I'm getting a beer," Nick said, and disappeared through the archway leading to the rest of the apartment.

Amanda picked up her garment bag, prepared to flee as soon as he returned. She shouldn't have come here. This had nothing to do with their business arrangement, nothing to do with her goal of derailing the Wedding Ring. She'd given in to childish curiosity and now she regretted it.

Her nervous gaze skittered around, coming to rest on Nick's CD rack, crammed with what had to be hundreds of albums. She glanced in the direction of the kitchen—he was taking an awfully long time opening one bottle of beer—and started perusing his music collection. He owned an impressive assortment of classic rock, plus several albums that didn't fit neatly into any category, such as the fiddle music that had been playing when she'd arrived.

A disk caught her eye. The Temptations. Amanda smiled. She ran her finger along the spines of the jewel box CD cases in that section of the rack. Stevie Wonder. The Four Tops. Diana Ross and the Supremes. The Commodores.

With her free hand she pulled out a Marvin Gaye album, flipped over the jewel box and scanned the list of songs, hearing the lyrics in her head.

"Aha." Nick's voice yanked her back to the here and now. "The lady's a closet Motown fan."

Amanda realized with chagrin that she'd been bopping to music only she could hear, sort of dancing in place. She slipped the CD case back in its slot.

"So much for you being an aficionada of classical music." He set two drinks—a glass of beer and orange juice on ice—on the coffee table, along with a bowl of honey-mustard pretzels.

"I never claimed to be any kind of an expert," she said as he took the garment bag from her and tossed it back on the sofa, "but I do like classical."

"How often do you listen to it?"

"I...I listen to it. I mean, I don't play music all the time like you do. Sometimes I like it to be dead quiet so I can curl up with a good book."

"'A good book' meaning one of the classics, right? Ms. Coppersmith wouldn't be caught dead curling up with the latest paperback page-turner." He handed her the glass of juice. "At least she wouldn't admit to it."

"You really do think I'm some kind of elitist snob, don't you?"

"No. What I think is that you've cultivated a particular image, and you're trying hard to live up to it."

"That's worse. I'd rather be thought of as elitist than a fraud."

"You aren't either, actually. You're just a little insecure."

Amanda set down her juice without tasting it. "I'm leaving."

Nick retrieved the album she'd been looking at. He removed the Eileen Ivers CD from the stereo and popped in the Marvin Gaye disk. "I know which song you were playing in your head." He pushed the play button, advanced to the cut he wanted and adjusted the volume. "I could tell by the way your hips were wiggling."

"I said I'm leaving." Amanda turned to grab the garment bag and her purse, but Nick was faster. He spun her into his arms just as the speakers pumped out the throbbing instrumental lead-in to "Heard It Through the Grapevine."

How had he known?

The music was hypnotic. Amanda found it impossible to be still with the song's irresistibly earthy beat pulsing through her—and with Nick leading her with surprising grace and skill.

He flicked a glance to her high-heeled pumps. "Get rid of them."

She kicked off her shoes, and so did he. A willowy five-seven, Amanda always thought of herself as tall, but being barefoot magnified the height difference between her and Nick. At that moment she felt downright petite.

And it wasn't simply his height, which, at just under six feet, wasn't all that lofty. Nick possessed a presence that few men could claim. He garnered people's notice and, more important, their respect. People tended to listen to Nick. Some might call it charisma.

Whatever it was, Amanda wasn't altogether comfortable with it. She hadn't bargained on charisma when she'd hired a taxi driver to pretend to be her beau. She felt the reins of control slipping inch by inch from her fingers, and she didn't like it one bit.

There was no question that Nick was in control now, shoving the coffee table and sofa toward the wall, swiftly rolling the rug out of the way, clearing dance space on the gleaming hardwood floor in all of about five seconds. Then she was back in his arms, dancing to the magnetic tune, which urged her to move her hips in a way that could only be called inviting.

She couldn't *not* move her hips that way. Not with this song. Damn that Marvin Gaye, anyway.

Nick was masterful, whirling her out, reeling her in, spinning her under his arm, smoothly switching hands as he guided her movements. She'd never considered herself much of a dancer, but with him leading, it was effortless. He'd cleared plenty of space, making Amanda thankful for her short hem and the uninhibited range of motion it afforded. The polished oak floor felt cool and glassy under her stockinged feet. After about half a minute she was so warm she had to toss off her pale blue suit jacket and push up the sleeves of her ivory silk blouse.

When the song ended she was actually disappointed—but not for long. As she upended the frosty glass of orange juice and drained it, Nick started playing another song of Marvin's, "Got to Give It Up," followed by several more high-energy Motown hits:

Stevie Wonder's "Superstition," "The Tears of a Clown," by Smokey Robinson and the Miracles, Thelma Houston's "Don't Leave Me This Way," and "Give It to Me, Baby," by Rick James.

They danced to every one.

Amanda had always loved this kind of music, on a gut level that was hard to explain. So why didn't she own any Motown albums? Was it true what Nick had said? Was she one big put-on, a bundle of insecurities obsessed with appearances? The thought that he saw her that way embarrassed her, and it shouldn't.

He was the hired help, after all. She shouldn't care what he thought of her.

Amanda was ready to collapse, but Nick wasn't even winded. When he placed a fresh CD in the stereo, she signaled wearily that she'd had enough, and commenced a controlled fall with her butt aimed at the sofa.

Nick seized her arms before she made contact and pulled her back onto the makeshift dance floor. She began to groan pitifully until she recognized the languid strains of "Just My Imagination Running Away with Me," by the Temptations. Too tuckered out to object, she allowed him to hold her close. Gradually the slow, sweet tune melted any last shreds of resistance and she leaned into him, rested her head on his shoulder and swayed with him to the music.

"This is a good one to cool down to," he murmured into her hair.

"Mmm..." Amanda let her eyes drift half-closed, let Nick saturate her senses. His humid warmth seeped into her, teasing her nostrils with the clean, appealing scent of his exertions, layered over the lingering woodsy fragrance of soap. She felt the strong, steady beat of his heart against her own chest. His powerful arms surrounded her, supported her. Protected her.

That was how she felt at that moment, as exhaustion liquified her brain and turned her limbs to oatmeal. Protected. Cherished.

Not alone.

It was a tantalizing sensation for Amanda, more seductive than sex, more irresistible than a ten-course feast to a starving woman. Greedily she soaked up this extraordinary feeling, absorbing every scrap of it, recognizing it for the fleeting thing it was. At least for her.

As she and Nick shuffled together in a slow circle, the words of the song penetrated her fuzzy mind. She'd never realized before how poignant the lyrics were, telling the story of a man dreaming of a future with the woman he loves. The man tells himself how lucky he is, and that he will surely die if someone takes her from him. But it turns out that it really is just a dream—his imagination running away with him. Because in reality, "she doesn't even know me."

Amanda's eyes opened. *She doesn't even know me.*

She wondered whether Nick chose this song for its lyrics, as a statement, and decided she didn't want to know. He mustn't think of her that way. She mustn't let him.

His big hand pushed aside her hair to slide over her nape and cup it. Amanda felt the leashed power in his warm, rough fingers as he tilted her head up. His eyes were more intense than she'd ever seen them, darkly penetrating. Her gaze fluttered to his mouth. Was he going to kiss her?

She mustn't allow it, she knew that, even as every nerve in her body hummed in anticipation. It was as if some kind of magnetic force pulled her to him.

Raising her eyes to his, she saw desire and indecision, saw him struggling with his own headstrong impulses.

And she saw the instant sanity prevailed. His gaze sharpened as he pulled back to a safer emotional distance.

It all happened in the blink of an eye, but it left Amanda shaken. A surge of adrenaline snuffed out the last of her dreamy languor and revved her pulse.

What almost happened here? Had she imagined it?

Watching Nick now, as she stepped away from him, hastily scooped up her purse and garment bag and mumbled an awkward goodbye, she decided that yes, she had indeed imagined it. She must have. His expression now was blandly neutral. No heated looks. No almost-kiss. *Just my imagination,* she thought.

Running away with me.

6

"LET ME *GUESS*," a throaty female voice purred.

Nick turned from the bar, two fresh drinks in hand, to find himself cornered by the leather-clad dominatrix who'd been eyeing him all evening.

Having driven a cab in New York for six years, Nick had thought he'd seen everything. That was before he and Amanda had arrived at the private Halloween costume party being held at Hunter's comedy club, Stitches, where most of the two hundred or so guests appeared to be vying for most outrageous costume—with attitude to match. By comparison, Nick and Amanda's Samson and Delilah outfits belonged in Sunday school.

The club was a study in controlled chaos, the food and top-shelf booze abundant, the dance band loud and energetic, and the decorations delightfully over-done, including all those pumpkins he and Amanda had helped pick three days earlier, now standing sentry as hilariously gruesome jack-o'-lanterns.

The dominatrix would have been tall even without her stratospheric high-heeled mules, the perfect accompaniment to her black fishnet stockings and a studded leather push-up corset that would have made the Marquis de Sade weep for joy. She sported painful-looking piercings in a variety of body parts that were visible and, he had little doubt, in a few that weren't. The lethal-looking cat-o'-nine-tails that she stroked over his chest appeared a bit frayed, making Nick wonder if her search for a costume had ended at her bedroom closet.

She pressed closer in the crush of partygoers, crowding him against the bar, enveloping him in a fog of heavy, musky perfume. "You're a Roman *centurion*, aren't you?" She gave him a lingering once-over, her hungry gaze zeroing in on his legs, bare below the thigh-length tunic except where the leather thongs of his sandals crisscrossed his calves.

"But you've been defeated in *battle*, haven't you?" she said. "Now you're held *captive*. They've taken your helmet, your shield and your *sword*. And put you in *these*." She tugged hard on the fake manacles that encircled his wrists. Pellegrino water sloshed out of the goblet in his right hand, and he nearly lost his grip on the slippery beer glass in his left.

He said, "Uh, listen, I've gotta go find my—"

"All that brute strength of yours *shackled*. Ruthlessly *imprisoned*." Her heavily made-up eyes glittered as her talon-tipped fingernails raked his biceps.

"Ow!" If he hadn't been holding the drinks, he might have been able to peel her off of him.

"How *humiliating* it must be, for a man of such obvious *potency*, such *virility*—" her voice was now a breathless growl "—to be chained like an *animal*, controlled, *forced* to do things against his *will*." She stared at him evenly as she added, "Wicked, *wicked* things.

What's this?" She grabbed the pair of sunglasses that he'd hooked onto his belt.

He said, "Uh, can I have those—"

"Since when do Roman centurions wear *shades?*"

She looked very cross. Nick kept one eye on her whip as he explained, "I'm Samson."

"What?"

"I'm supposed to be Samson, not a centurion. You know, Samson and Delilah?"

The cat-o'-nine-tails whooshed through the air and struck the bar next to him with a menacing *thwack!* "You told me you're a *centurion!*"

"Well, no, I didn't. You guessed—"

"Samson had *hair*. Lots and *lots* of hair."

"Yeah, and then he got a trim. Get it?" Nick lifted the drinks, indicating his manacles.

She put on his sunglasses. He had to admit, they went better with her getup than his. "Do you know what happens to naughty, *naughty* Samsons with very little hair who pretend to be Roman *centurions?*"

He snorted. "I can imagine."

She offered a wry smile and retrieved something from her ample cleavage. A business card, flamboyant crimson lettering on gold card stock. "If you'd like to do more than *imagine...*" She tucked the card into his belt. "Leave Delilah at *home.*"

Resignedly he said, "You're not going to give me back my sunglasses, are you?"

"You'll have to come get them." She leaned forward, and just when he'd decided she was going to kiss his cheek, she bit his earlobe. Hard.

"Ow! Stop that!"

"We'll work on your pain *threshold*."

"Sounds like fun," Amanda said, suddenly materializing to Nick's left. "Too bad I'm not invited."

Nick could only swallow his groan and wonder how much she'd heard. Nodding toward the dominatrix, he offered a strained chuckle. "Great costume, huh?"

Amanda coolly plucked the card out of his belt, glanced at it and handed it back to the lady. "Save it for some other *potent, virile* captive. This one's not *interested*."

The lady disappeared through the crowd, but not before mocking Amanda's possessive display with a feline hiss and a clawing gesture.

Nick handed her the goblet of Pellegrino water. "I was going to go look for you, but I couldn't get away from..." He shrugged and took a sip of his beer.

And nearly choked on it when Amanda said, "Madame Hertz. That's her name. *H-e-r-t-z*."

"You made that up."

"Says it right there on her card. Along with her address, phone, fax and cell numbers, e-mail address and Web site. Yeah," she added dryly, "great 'costume.'"

"Your jealousy is flattering."

"Oh, please." Amanda glanced around and lowered her voice. "It's all part of the act. Do you know any woman who'd stand by and watch some trollop crawl all over her man and not do something about it?"

"Well, you're a hell of an actress."

"I had to make it convincing. What's the matter? You wanted to keep her card? You were looking forward to paying a visit to Madame Hertz and learning all about tough love? Maybe you're already into that stuff and could teach her a thing or two."

"I thought we only needed to pretend for your close friends. Is that charming lady one of them?"

"Of course not! But I figure Hunter or Raven must know her. Who knows what she might tell them? We have to stay in character. You know, like a couple."

"I guess you're right." Nick slipped his arm around Amanda's waist. Pulling her closer, he nuzzled her temple, nosing aside one of the beaded tassels dangling from the gold-colored ornamental band encircling her forehead. "You look incredibly sexy in this outfit. Do you know that?"

The filmy, low-cut dress, with its gold trim and body-hugging cut, bore no resemblance to the tailored suits she wore to work. Of course, the giant pair of fake scissors hanging from her belt didn't contribute much to her allure, but it beat him having to wear that hideous wig. Insinuating his hand under the gold-shot teal cape, he rubbed her back in lazy circles.

She tensed. "What—what are you doing?"

"What you said," he murmured close to her ear. "Staying in character. Putting on a show for your nosy friends. And their nosy friends. And anyone *they* might know. We can't be too careful."

"All right, well, I think that's enough." Amanda

eased out of his arms. "For the time being." She sipped her drink.

The fact was, no one was paying a whole lot of attention to the two of them just then—everyone was too busy having a good time. Glancing toward the dance floor that had been set up near the stage, Nick spotted Grant and Charli trying to follow the steps of a complex line dance. The problem was, their clothing got in the way. No stranger to the domestic arts, Charli had sewn the padded costumes herself: she was a fast-food cheeseburger and he was a super-size order of fries.

Hunter was up on the wooden stage where he normally introduced comedians, including his wife, Raven, who regularly performed her amateur stand-up act on "open mike" nights. Tonight he'd been joined by Pippi Longstocking and Toulouse-Lautrec, the three of them leading his guests in the intricate steps of the line dance. Tonight Hunter was an ancient Egyptian, with a colorful, shoulder-length headdress and one of those short white things that wrapped around his hips, leaving his chest bare. With his dark, collar-length hair and residual suntan, he looked the part.

Casting his gaze toward the buffet tables, Nick spied Sunny and Kirk. Sunny was ethereally lovely in an authentic-looking medieval gown, while her husband had eschewed historical elegance in favor of Hollywood hype. Kirk was the Towering Inferno, from the old disaster movie of that name. The costume was as simple as it was original. He'd draped his long body in strips of red, yellow and orange felt that had been layered and slashed to look like flames consuming a skyscraper. The crowning touch was the tiny toy helicopter perched atop his blond head.

Nick watched Raven greet the couple as she piled a mountain of food on her plate. She'd used her five-months-pregnant belly to advantage when designing her costume, consisting of a black bodysuit adorned with yellow diagonal stripes: a highway speed bump.

Steering Amanda away from the bustle of activity around the bar, Nick headed for a deserted corner. "You seem really uptight tonight," he said, once they were away from prying ears. "Is it something I've done?"

Like almost kiss you last night at my place? He knew she'd never bring it up. To do so would be to acknowledge their mutual attraction. Not only did that attraction have no part in her game plan, it obviously scared the hell out of her. Nick didn't think it was him. He'd never given her reason to fear him. For some reason, the more they got to know each other, the more she resisted her own feelings for him.

And she did feel something for him. What, precisely, he wasn't sure. Perhaps just the age-old chemical thing, maybe something more. It would be helpful to *his* game plan if he could figure that one out.

Instead of answering his question directly, Amanda said, "You've been asking my friends about me. I want it to stop."

"Stop talking to your friends? Isn't that what I'm supposed—"

"Stop pumping them for information about me!" Amanda snapped, then belatedly checked to make sure no other guests were within earshot.

"I always thought a guy was expected to show a healthy interest in his ladylove. What exactly am I doing that's so terrible?"

"You know what you're doing. Asking about my interests, my upbringing, my family..." She looked him in the eye. "My ex-husbands."

"Amanda, I don't know what you imagine my sins are, but what we're talking about here is just idle conversation between me and your friends. I never pumped anyone for information. Did someone tell you I did?"

"Not... You're too clever to make it obvious. The fact is, you have no business trying to find out things about me."

"Why? Do you have some deep, dark secrets?"

"That's not the point. You have no right. It's not your place."

That last remark was clearly meant to remind him he was the lowly hired help, but somehow it sounded more calculated than spontaneous. She reinforced it with a fixed stare, which he returned steadily until she finally dragged her gaze away.

Nick couldn't dredge up anything resembling indignation. During the past three weeks he'd come to realize that Amanda hadn't been lying when she'd claimed not to be an elitist snob. He knew, too, that her current objective wasn't to grind him under her thumb, but rather to keep him at a distance the only way she knew how: by harping on the rules of conduct in their employer-employee relationship.

And by obsessively guarding her privacy. Nick could honestly say he hadn't crossed the line in his discussions with Sunny, Raven, Charli and their husbands. Nick was a people person—and a man of many talents, as he'd told Amanda. If it was true that he was coaxing information out of Amanda's pals, it was also true that he was skilled and charming and, yes, clever enough to do so subtly, without being considered pushy or rude. Amanda was overreacting.

She was doing everything in her power to disavow her attraction to him and keep him at arm's length, and he couldn't help but wonder why. He knew plenty of people who'd gone through divorces—sometimes more than one. Bottom line: it sucked and then you got over it, got on with your life. You didn't resort to Byzantine machinations to avoid risking another serious relationship.

Not unless you were Amanda Coppersmith.

Amanda placed her half-empty glass on the tray of a passing waiter, who, at six foot five and 250 pounds easy, was dressed as a belly dancer, complete with a long, platinum-blond wig and body hair in the simian range.

She faced Nick squarely. "I've put up with nosy friends my whole life, because I happen to love them and they put up with plenty from me in return. Let me be blunt."

"You?" He couldn't resist tweaking her. "The mistress of tact?"

"You are not my friend," she said. "Our association is strictly a business arrangement, and a temporary one at that. If you can manage to keep that in mind, *if* you can do the simple job you've been hired to do and keep your nose out of my personal life while you're doing it, then you and I will get along just fine. *Plus*—" she raised a finger "—your restraint will earn you a fifty percent bonus. *If*, on the other hand, you persist in the direction you've been going, I'll call a halt to the whole thing and all you walk away with is the two-hundred-dollar advance I've already paid."

Which he'd already spent on her birthday gift. She didn't say it, and neither did he. But of the two of them, only he knew that he wasn't in this for the salary she was offering. Not since day one. He had his eye on a hell of a lot more than payment for services rendered.

"Well?" she said when he didn't respond.

"If you fire me, are you going to go through the same stupid farce with someone else?"

"I am, only next time I'll be more careful who I cast in the role of Romeo."

Nick scrubbed a hand over his jaw. "I guess you're counting on your pals not catching on."

"Why should they? They don't seem at all suspicious of our relationship. They won't be next time, either."

"Well, unless someone clues them in."

Amanda's eyes narrowed dangerously. "What are you saying?"

He offered a nonchalant shrug. "You don't think

your lifelong friends, who you say you love so much, would be interested in hearing how you duped them, played them all for fools?" He placed his palm on his chest. "Personally, I think they'd be very interested. Might make it a little hard to run the same scam on them again, though."

Her jaw worked silently. "How much do you want?"

"What, you think I'm trying to shake you down? We already have a deal. I'm not a greedy guy."

"Then why are you doing this?" Her silver eyes burned with an icy flame. "Just to show me who's in charge? To make the 'control freak' squirm a little?"

"That's just an added bonus. The fact is, you're changing the rules of this thing in midstream, and I don't like it."

Amanda advanced on him until mere inches separated them. Her hands were balled into fists at her sides. "I'm not changing anything. You were hired to play a role, nothing more. Certainly not to pry into my personal life."

"Like I said before, it's a little hard to pretend everlasting love when you know hardly anything about the lady in question. Have you thought that maybe I'm just trying to fill in the blanks so your meddlesome friends don't get suspicious?"

"I'm not buying that one anymore. You've had your warning. I'm not impressed by your threat, but if it will keep you focused, I'll up the ante. Two thousand dollars. Payable when we tragically break up following a brief but heartfelt engagement. This discussion is now over."

She ensured it by stomping off. Nick watched her stiff back until she disappeared into the throng of guests. Within moments he became aware of another person separating from a nearby knot of people and approaching him. He prayed it wasn't Madame Hertz and her cat-o'-nine-tails, and was immensely relieved to hear a familiar deep voice, now tinged with sarcasm.

"Looks like that went well."

Nick looked and saw that he'd been joined by Pinocchio. Every detail was there, from the short pants and suspenders to the painted-on elbow and knee joints to the full-head mask, complete with the signature lie-detector schnozz and pointy cap. Only this Pinocchio was about six feet tall.

"You're a very disturbing sight," Nick said. "You know that, don't you?"

"It came down to this or one of those space aliens with the big eyes. I figured this would be more comfortable," Pinocchio said, indicating the shorts and short-sleeved shirt. "Amanda didn't look like she was too thrilled with you just now. Is she getting suspicious?"

"Nah, it's just these hang-ups of hers. I'm having a little trouble getting past them."

"Nothing you weren't warned about from the get-go."

"All you told me was that she was skittish after a

couple of divorces," Nick said. "This lady has built a wall a Sherman tank couldn't get through."

"You don't sound too optimistic. I'm beginning to think you might not be the right choice for this particular undertaking."

Nick had known this guy for eight years, long enough to recognize this unsubtle manipulation for what it was. He refused to rise to the bait. "There's no one better suited than me, and you know it. I just wish I had more time."

"Time's something I can't help you with. We're locked in. Just do whatever you have to, to make it happen, and then we'll all get what we want." Pinocchio glanced at Nick. "Unless you blow your cover first."

"Don't worry about that. As far as Amanda is concerned, I'm a blue-collar drone out to make a quick buck. Speaking of which, she doubled my 'salary.' All I have to do is play my part like a good little boy and not ask too many uncomfortable questions. Can you believe that? As if I'd be satisfied with two grand."

"It doesn't surprise me. Just keep the final goal in mind. And remember, it was my recommendation that got you this gig. Try not to blow it."

"Your faith in me is touching."

Pinocchio slapped Nick on the back. "Whatever you do, just let her keep thinking she's in control."

7

AMANDA'S DIRECT LINE rang as she was hurriedly stuffing work papers into her Louis Vuitton briefcase, one foot practically out the door. Her instinct was to ignore it, but then she realized it could be her mom again. She snatched up the receiver. "Amanda Coppersmith."

"You sound out of breath."

"Nick, I can't talk. I'm on my way out." She glanced at the huge picture windows in her corner office; the snow was coming down harder.

"What's wrong?"

She forced calm into her voice. "Nothing's wrong. I'm in a hurry, so—"

"Don't BS me. What is it?"

"Well, if you must know—" Amanda shut her briefcase "—it's personal. A family matter. So thanks for your concern, but—"

"I'll be there in two minutes."

"What?"

"I'm right around the corner. I'll pick you up in front of your building."

"No, you won't. I'm going to grab a cab."

"That's right—mine."

"Oh, for heaven's sake, Nick, I don't have time to argue with you—"

"Good." *Click.*

Precisely one minute and twenty-six seconds later, Amanda was power-walking west on Twentieth Street toward Sixth Avenue to catch a ride uptown when a yellow taxi barreled around the corner. She might not have recognized Nick's vehicle, but there was no mistaking his driving style, the smooth, tight, self-assured maneuvers, even at that hellish speed and on those slick roads.

He stopped right next to her and rolled down the driver's window. "Get in."

"Don't be ridiculous, Nick." Amanda's breath smoked in the cold air. She snugged the collar of her eggplant-colored microfiber trench coat around her throat. "This isn't your problem."

"I never said it was. Can't you accept a lift from a friend?"

His words were an unpleasant reminder of their conversation a month earlier during the Halloween party. *You are not my friend. Our association is strictly a business arrangement.*

True words, words that had needed to be said, for many reasons. But that didn't keep her from cringing whenever she thought about them. Yet here was Nick offering her a ride. As a friend.

Snowflakes clung to Amanda's eyelashes as she scanned the traffic visible on Sixth. She didn't see any taxis with their rooftop license-number lights on.

Nick gave voice to her thoughts. "Good luck catching a cab in this weather. Plus rush hour's getting an early start. You know how it is on Fridays."

Amanda slumped in defeat, knowing she had little choice in the matter. Yanking open the back passenger door and sliding inside, she said, "But you have to put the meter on."

"Sure thing." Nick pulled away from the curb. He did not put the meter on. After a few moments he said, "It would help if you told me where we're going."

She muttered, "Eighty-sixth between Lex and Third."

"What's up there?"

The Coppersmith family soap opera, she thought. *Move over, Jerry Springer.*

Nick glanced at her in the rearview mirror, his eyes now a rich dark brown, and too insightful for comfort. "The silent treatment, huh? Now, let's see. What topics of discussion cause the lady to clam up?"

She emitted a loud, exasperated sigh.

"There's your marital history, for starters," he said. "Does one of your exes happen to live on East Eighty-sixth?"

"Shut up, Nick."

"Did he call you up and plead with you to take him back? Beg your forgiveness for whatever made you walk out on him in the first place?"

She hadn't seen that one coming. Amanda knew that the wrenching pain of it was there, on her face, for the fleeting instant their eyes met in the mirror. She directed her gaze out the window, too late.

Everyone always assumed the same thing. And

why not? How easy it must be to imagine Amanda Coppersmith, frosty bitch boss, walking out on two husbands in succession without a backward glance.

Fine with her. Let them all think of her as some kind of damn Ice Queen. Anything was better than the humiliating truth.

Nick remained silent while he navigated the streets of Manhattan, heading east on Twentieth before turning north on Park Avenue. Snowflakes did their little dance of death into the relentless whoosh-whoosh of the windshield wipers. Traffic built steadily as rush hour got under way.

Nick started humming. Amanda recognized the tune, and her mind supplied the lyrics. She could almost hear James Taylor's honeyed voice singing about the first of December being covered with snow.

She smiled. Today was the first of December. And it was covered with snow.

She shook her head in wonder. Nick had gotten her to smile. A small miracle in her present frame of mind. How had he managed that?

Amanda took a deep breath. She relaxed against the chilly backrest, only then becoming aware of how stiffly she'd been holding her body.

She wiped condensation from the window and peered out at Park Avenue, at the ceaseless tide of pedestrians, at the Waldorf-Astoria, majestic against a gunmetal sky aswirl in snowflakes. She looked at the back of Nick's head, and at the picture on his hack license, mounted just behind him. She recalled the first time she'd seen that picture. All she'd known about

Nick then was that he quoted dead earls and didn't smile for license photos.

Now she knew that he was willing to hum a silly old song to bring a smile to *her* face.

"It's my parents," she said.

Nick's eyes flicked to her in the rearview. He didn't say anything.

"Do you remember..." Amanda's throat tried to close up. Damn it! Why couldn't she just care less? Like Jared. Her brother didn't understand her insistence on privacy, didn't understand the need to keep things under wraps.

She started over. "Do you remember the night of my birthday party, when...you know, my parents weren't there and I said they had a wedding to go to?"

Nick nodded, his eyes on the road. He didn't leap on that as he could have, didn't taunt her for waiting so long to come clean when he'd known all along she was lying.

"Well, the thing is...my mom and dad..." She couldn't even say it.

She didn't have to; Nick did it for her. "They split up."

It sounded so simple, the way he said it, so straightforward. She nodded, knowing he wasn't looking at her at that moment, not caring. She wasn't answering him; she was confirming the truth for herself.

Amanda pulled off one cashmere-lined leather glove, extracted a tissue from a small pack in her briefcase and blotted her eyes. "You'd think with my 'marital history,' as you put it, this wouldn't bother me so much."

Watching the rearview mirror, she saw a gentle smile crease Nick's face, though he never took his eyes off the road. "It's your folks, Amanda. You're allowed to be upset."

"Yeah, well, Jared seems to be taking it in stride."

"Why do you say that? Because he's not sobbing and tearing out his hair? Men hold a lot inside—you know that. I'll bet if you asked Noelle, you'd find out it's getting to your brother as much as it's getting to you, he just doesn't show it the same way."

"Well...maybe you're right. I had a hard time persuading him to keep a lid on all this, though. He sees no reason it shouldn't be public knowledge."

"Why are you keeping it secret?" he asked. "Everyone will find out eventually."

"They might not have to. This separation might not last. Mom and Dad could get back together. Why should this little...hiatus be anyone else's business?"

"I don't think you're giving your friends enough credit, Amanda. I mean, people break up, sometimes after decades of marriage. It happens. Raven and Charli and the rest of them are mature, compassionate people. Don't assume they'll think less of your folks because of this."

"I know you think I'm obsessed with appearances, but that isn't it. I just..." She sighed. "I keep hoping I'll wake up and discover this was all a bad dream."

"How long ago did they split up?"

"Around Labor Day."

"Three months," he said. "Pretty long for a bad dream."

"You're saying it's time I faced the unpleasant truth. Stopped deluding myself into thinking it'll blow over."

"No, I'm saying you should remember what close friends are for. You're going through something intense here—you're grieving, in a sense. Share it with Sunny and Raven and Charli. They love you. Let them help you through it."

Amanda thought back to last year when she was going through her second divorce, and the paralyzing depression she'd suffered. How different would that experience have been if she'd known Nick then, if he'd given her this same advice and she'd heeded it? If she'd let the people who loved her know the full extent of what she was going through? If she hadn't felt the need to show the world how tough and self-reliant she was?

Because she'd learned the hard way she wasn't all that tough.

"So who lives on East Eighty-sixth?" Nick asked. "Your dad?"

"My mother. When their...troubles came to a head, she moved into this apartment owned by a friend of hers who's in Paris this whole year on business."

They passed the remainder of the drive in silence. Nick didn't ask what was so urgent that she'd had to bolt out of the office early to see her mother. Finally he turned onto Eighty-sixth and Amanda directed him to a fashionable high-rise apartment building.

"Thanks, Nick. Don't wait for me—I could be a while."

"Of course I'll wait for you."

"Don't be silly. I'll grab a cab to Penn Station later. You're working! You've wasted enough time on me."

"I offered you a lift, Amanda. That means both ways."

Stubborn man. With relief she saw that the street was lined with parked cars. "Well, suit yourself, but you'll have to sit out here double-parked. And I might be a while. What are you doing? You can't get in here."

"Says who?" Nick asked, already in the process of parallel parking. Looking over his shoulder, he palmed the wheel with one hand, expertly shoehorning the taxi into a spot that Amanda would have sworn was about a foot shorter than the vehicle. He killed the engine and they both got out.

Amanda sighed. "Would it do me any good to ask you to wait downstairs in the lobby while I go up?"

"None at all," he replied pleasantly.

Inside the building, the doorman called up to Apartment 18E to let Mrs. Coppersmith know she had visitors. Amanda and Nick shared most of the elevator ride to the eighteenth floor with a tall, bald man and his tiny papillon puppy, both of them dusted with melting snow.

Nick stood close to Amanda as she rang the bell to her mother's apartment. Perhaps he sensed her trepidation. She thought she was concealing it well, but Nick always seemed to have the uncanny ability to see through her serene facade. The aura of quiet strength he exuded bolstered her confidence.

It reminded her of that night when they'd slow-danced in his apartment to "Just My Imagination Running Away with Me"—a song she hadn't been able to get out of her head since. She'd felt protected then, and that feeling was now amplified tenfold as she listened to hurried footsteps approach on the other side of the door.

Suddenly she was grateful to Nick for not letting her come up here alone.

The door swung open and there was Mom, looking harried but beautiful as always, and much younger than her fifty-three years. Her skin was smooth and unblemished, her hair the same silky ash-blond it had been since childhood, even if nowadays it got a little help from her hairdresser. The raw silk sweater and designer jeans she wore were size six, and at five-eight, she was an inch taller than her daughter.

"Mandy!" She cast a nervous glance out into the hallway and lowered her voice. "I'm so glad you're here." She stood aside so they could enter the small foyer.

"Mom, this is my friend Nick. He, uh, gave me a ride up here."

They shook hands. Nick said, "It's a pleasure to meet you, Mrs. Coppersmith."

"Please. Call me Liv. Mandy, I'm so sorry to make you come all the way up here. I'm just...I'm at the end of my rope. I didn't know what else to do."

"Where is he now?" Amanda stepped into the living room, decorated in boring shades of beige and taupe that her mother chose to refer to as "stone," "mushroom" and "desert."

"I don't know. Connor went out right after I called you. We had this horrible fight."

Amanda turned to Nick, knowing some kind of explanation was called for. "Connor is my mother's..." She couldn't bring herself to say "boyfriend."

"I get the picture." Turning to Amanda's mother, Nick cut to the chase. "Has he hit you?"

"He...he shoves me around. It's getting worse."

"Mom!" Amanda grabbed her mother's shoulders; she searched her face for signs of violence. "Why didn't you tell me?"

"I couldn't. I was so ashamed. After I went on about how wonderful he was, how well he treated me. Then he started changing, and at first I thought, well, it has to be me."

Nick said, "You want him out of your life."

"Yes, but it's not that easy."

"He's been bullying her," Amanda explained. "Threatening her."

"Does he have keys to the apartment?" he asked.

Amanda hadn't even thought of that. She bit back a groan when her mother nodded miserably. *Oh, Mom. What were you thinking?*

"He was so charming." Liv's eyes filled with tears. "I know you don't believe it. You think I'm some silly old besotted woman whose head was turned by a younger man.... But he was—he was so sweet, so sincere. He made me feel special."

Nick asked, "How much has he taken you for?"

Amanda was about to tell him *No, it's not like that, my mother's not that stupid,* but one look at Liv's face and the words died on a whimper. "Oh, Mom, tell me you didn't give him money."

"A short-term loan, he said. Only until his Christmas bonus came through. He wanted to take us on a cruise."

Nick said, "He's got a job, then?"

Liv shook her head. "He told me he was national sales manager of Waterford USA. When I realized he didn't know hand-cut lead crystal from pressed glass, I called Waterford and discovered they'd never heard of him."

"How much?" Nick repeated.

Liv closed her eyes and rubbed her forehead. "Sixteen thousand."

Amanda's jaw dropped. Nick gestured for her to restrain herself. She turned away for a moment, took a few deep breaths.

"Mandy, I'm so sorry." Liv was weeping now. "I've made such a mess of things. I *am* a foolish old woman."

"No, you're not." Nick's voice was firm. "You've been taken in by a con artist, Liv. These guys have no conscience. They prey on people's vulnerabilities."

Liv's tears flowed freely now. "If Perry weren't such a stiff-necked, self-absorbed—"

Amanda advanced on her mother. "Don't you dare blame this on Dad!"

Nick placed a calming hand on Amanda's shoulder. She shook it off and backed away from Liv. She knew she should feel humiliated, having an outsider witness this sordid scene, but at the moment more pressing concerns overwhelmed her.

Sixteen thousand dollars. Gone. She couldn't imagine how they'd go about getting it back. As for Connor having keys to the apartment, she'd have to call a locksmith, get the locks changed. But that wouldn't stop the harassment. Maybe Amanda could persuade Liv to move in with her for a while. They might have to get a restraining order against Connor, though she doubted it would have the desired effect. She'd met the guy. He didn't seem the type to comply with a piece of paper ordering him to stay away from an emotionally fragile woman with a plump checkbook.

"Your father will never take me back now," Liv said, her expression more bleak than Amanda had ever seen it.

"Do you want him to?" Amanda felt the stirring of hope.

"I never realized what I was giving up until..." Liv wrapped her arms around herself. "But it's too late now. After my foolish behavior."

"Maybe not." Amanda put her arms around her mother and held her tight. "I have a feeling Dad might be more forgiving than you think." She'd brought turkey and pumpkin pie to her father on Thanksgiving Day last week, and she'd never seen him more lonely and miserable. She suspected that only that asinine pride of his kept him from taking the first step and reconciling with his wife.

The sound of a key turning in the lock galvanized them all. Liv flinched and took a step back. Amanda steeled herself for the coming confrontation.

Nick reached the door in a couple of long strides just as it opened. "Connor! How's it goin'?" he said in greeting, all smiles, his hand out as if to bestow a hearty handshake.

Connor stood in the entryway, blinking at the stranger, for the split second it took Nick to snatch his key ring out of his hand. "Hey!" He tried to grab it back, but Nick neatly sidestepped him while he separated the smaller ring with Liv's apartment keys from the larger ring, which he returned to Connor with a negligent toss.

"Those are mine!" Connor lunged at Nick. They were about the same height and age, but Connor was beefier, his hard body thick with bulging muscles he maintained through daily workouts at a health club. He was strong, but he didn't count on his opponent's speed and agility. Faster than Amanda could take it in, Nick had the other man in a headlock from behind. Connor let out a howl and continued to struggle as Nick twisted his arm behind his back and pinned it there.

"I'd just as soon break it," Nick calmly informed him.

Connor responded with a string of raw curses. Nick

yanked upward on his arm. The curses died on a grunt of pain.

"Watch your language in front of the ladies. Now, you and I have a few things to discuss." To Amanda and her mother, Nick said, "We won't be long," before steering Connor down the hall and shoving him unceremoniously into the bedroom.

The door slammed shut. Amanda looked at her mother, who stared back, wide-eyed. The two of them tiptoed down the hall, listening intently. Connor's bellowing carried easily through the door; Amanda had to strain to hear Nick's muted but authoritative voice, too quiet and calm for her to make out specific words. Eventually Connor ran out of steam. Either that or whatever Nick was telling him made an impression. In any event, it wasn't long before the door opened, causing Amanda and her mother to scramble back to the living room.

"Connor and I are going to take a little ride," Nick said, buttoning his navy peacoat.

Connor, his sullen face a dull brick-red, refused to meet the women's eyes. Nick ushered him out the door, after telling Amanda he'd be back.

After a few moments of stunned silence, Amanda shrugged out of her coat and tossed it over a mushroom-colored love seat. "Do you still have that bottle of Absolut?"

"I think I can even scrounge up a few drops of vermouth and some olives."

One and a half martinis later, the doorman buzzed to inform them that Mr. Stephanos was on his way up.

Amanda met him at the door. She peered down the hallway. He was alone.

"What was that all that about?" she demanded.

Inside the apartment, he pulled a wad of money from his coat and handed it to Amanda's mother. "Thirteen thousand three hundred and seventeen. He spent the rest, but you'll have it by the end of next week."

Amanda stared in shock as Liv riffled the stack of bills: hundreds and fifties mainly. "He handed this over? Just like that?"

Nick showed her his dimple. "Just like that." It was clear that whatever he'd said or done to persuade Connor to return Liv's money, it was between him and that loathsome swindler. "He'll get the balance of the money to me and I'll deliver it to you, Liv. You'll never have to see him again."

Liv said, "You think he'll really leave me alone now?"

"I can pretty much guarantee it."

She sagged in relief. Tears of gratitude glazed her eyes. "Nick, I don't know what to say. I was—I couldn't—I can't—" Liv broke off on a damp chuckle. "I'm not all that articulate at the moment, but what I'm trying to say is thank you." She gave him a warm kiss on the cheek.

"You're very welcome." He looked at Amanda, and she knew he read it in her eyes, the relief, the gratitude, and more—those slippery, shadowy feelings she tried so hard to deny. At the moment she was incapable of sorting it all out, or holding any of it back.

"Thank you," she whispered around the tightness in her throat.

His expression softened, his velvety dark eyes searching her face, seeing too much, she knew. It seemed like forever before she managed to tear her gaze away. One look at her mother's astute smile and she knew that things had just gotten a lot more complicated.

Liv said, "Mandy, how come you haven't brought Nick around to meet me before now?"

"Well, we're not... I mean, we're just..." It was no use. Amanda and Nick were an official couple in the eyes of her Wedding Ring pals, as well as her brother, Jared. It was just a matter of time before her mother heard about Nick from one of them. Amanda felt the reins of control slip one more notch.

She glanced at Nick, who watched her in silence, waiting to take his cue from her.

"We haven't been seeing each other all that long," Amanda said. "Less than two months."

Liv chuckled. "Well, I don't think we'll forget this introduction anytime soon."

And won't it make a great story for our kids someday, Amanda thought with warped amusement. *How Daddy terrorized the gigolo Grandma was shacking up with.*

Whoa! Back up, girl!

"Our kids"? "Daddy"? Where had that come from? It had to be the one and a half martinis she'd downed.

He's not really your man! her mind screamed. *He never will be! Stop thinking of him that way!*

Although Nick had certainly handled this wretched situation as if he really were her man, as if he had a genuine stake in her happiness and the welfare of her family.

Amanda found herself wondering how Roger and Ben, her exes, would have responded in the same situation. Somehow she couldn't imagine either of them thoroughly intimidating someone like Connor without so much as raising his voice, as Nick had done. In fact, she couldn't imagine Roger or Ben even caring enough to intervene.

Liv was her old self once more, upbeat and sociable. "Let me take you two to dinner. Nick and I can get acquainted and I can ask him where he learned those fancy wrestling moves." Her eyes glowed with approval of her daughter's gentleman friend.

"I wish I could, Liv." Nick appeared genuinely regretful as he explained, "I have to get back to work."

Liv looked disappointed. "Another time, then. Soon. What kind of work do you do, Nick?"

He glanced at Amanda, and she could tell he wasn't happy having to deceive her mother; Liv had been deceived enough by that crook Connor. Amanda could no longer remember why it had once seemed so important to pretend that Nick was something he wasn't. She wouldn't have hesitated to tell Liv that he drove a taxi, but the truth was no longer an option; she had to maintain the pretense she'd constructed for the benefit of her Wedding Ring friends. Normally an honest person, Amanda felt mentally exhausted by all the subterfuge.

The least she could do for Nick, after what he'd just done for her, was to spare him having to look her mother in the eye and lie to her. Amanda made herself say, "Nick owns a fleet of limos."

This didn't appear to surprise Liv. "Well then, I can understand why you have to run, Nick. Which makes me all the more grateful that you took time out of your busy day to help me." She sent Amanda a look that said *You picked a good one this time.*

8

"YOU LIKE THE ZABAGLIONE?"

Amanda chewed back a grin watching Luisa Rossi, the ninety-three-year-old, black-clad matriarch of Charli's family, hover over Nick, armed with a bowl and serving spoon.

Nick smiled up at the old woman. "The zabaglione is wonderful, Mrs. Rossi! I've had two servings."

"Good boy. You have more." She started to ladle another helping into his dessert goblet.

He tried to wave her off, to no avail. "It's delicious," he said, "really, but I'm much too full...." He gave up, eyeing the huge mound of frothy, pale zabaglione that Mrs. Rossi had deposited in his goblet.

With her free hand, she patted his cheek. "It's light. You eat more. Keep you big and strong. Grant!" Abandoning Nick, she turned her attention to her granddaughter's husband. "You like the zabaglione?"

Amanda sat on one side of Nick at the Rossis' long dining table, Charli on the other. Charli leaned toward him and said, "You're too polite, Nick. She'll keep feeding you till we have to roll you out of here."

It was December 24 and the entire sprawling Rossi clan, plus assorted friends and neighbors, had convened at the home of Charli's parents for a traditional

Italian Christmas Eve dinner, heavy on the seafood. Following a feast that included stuffed squid braised in white wine, shellfish salad, baked striped bass, cold trout in orange marinade, sliced pasta roll with spinach filling, molded risotto, and Grandma Rossi's famous *gnocchi verdi*, the Rossi women brought out dessert: chocolate layer cake flavored with rum and coffee, apple fritters, macerated fruit, and the endless zabaglione. Plus gallons of hot, strong espresso and cappuccino.

Nick leaned back in his chair with a little groan. Amanda patted his shoulder. "I tried to tell you to pace yourself."

Having spent a good part of the past quarter century as a guest in this house, Amanda had long ago learned to do just that. No matter how much food Charli's mother or grandmother piled onto her plate, no matter how good everything tasted—and it was always heavenly—she forced herself to eat small bites and set down her fork between them. It was just too much food.

Nick, however, had failed to heed her advice. His eyes had popped at the mouthwatering spread and he'd dug in with gusto. Now, as he stared balefully at the zabaglione before him, Amanda decided to take pity.

"Come on." Rising, she picked up their espresso cups. "Let's find a quiet place to digest."

The cozy living room, a study in floral chintz, was currently dominated by an enormous artificial Christmas tree, groaning under too many glittery ornaments, garlands and tinsel, and hundreds of colored blinking lights. Amanda and Nick settled on the chintz-covered love seat and were soon joined by Charli, Raven, Sunny and their husbands. The other guests were dispersed throughout the small house: the men in the den watching a football-highlights program on ESPN, the women in the kitchen washing dishes and gossiping, and the kids playing Ping-Pong and board games in the basement playroom.

Sunny snuggled on her husband's lap on the chintz sofa, now devoid of its usual protective plastic cover in honor of the holiday. Amanda asked them how their recent trip to California went.

"It was great," Kirk said. "I'm so glad we did it. Ian got to spend time with Linda's parents, and they got to meet Sunny."

It must have been an emotional visit. Kirk's first wife, Linda, had died in an auto accident a year earlier, leaving their son, Ian, now almost two years old, motherless. Afterward Kirk had moved from California back to Long Island and renewed his relationship with Sunny Bleecker, his high school sweetheart and now the second Mrs. Kirk Larsen.

Sunny said, "Linda's folks were so sweet to me, so warm and open. When we left they thanked me for being such a good mother to their grandson." Her eyes were misty and she wore a little smile. "We've asked them to come out here for Easter."

Ian ran into the living room then, a miniature version of Kirk with his pale blond hair and lively blue eyes. "Nonni gimme shockit ship I-keam!" he announced. *Nonni*, Italian for "Grandma," was what Charli and her seven siblings called Mrs. Rossi.

"I can see that." Sunny grinned. "You're wearing most of it."

Ian looked down at his red pullover, now liberally decorated with chocolate chip ice cream, the youngster's all-time favorite dessert. He sang, "Uh-oh!"

Kirk said, "That's okay, champ. Uh-ohs happen. That's why we have a washing machine." The sticky stuff was all over the boy's face and hands as well. Kirk picked up a poinsettia-decorated cocktail napkin from the stack left on the coffee table. Beckoning Ian to him, he gently scrubbed his face. "There. Why don't you go downstairs. I think Janine's waiting to play Candy Land with you."

He didn't have to say it twice. Ian was off like a shot, headed for the door to the basement.

Raven, seven months pregnant now and quite rotund under her maroon maternity jumper, was ensconced in one of a pair of wing chairs. Hunter stood behind her, massaging her shoulders. Amanda asked her how she was feeling.

"Not bad, except I think the baby's playing soccer with that second helping of risotto I had."

Just then Amanda noticed a sudden rolling movement under Raven's jumper. Amanda gasped as Raven patted her stomach and said, "I think he got it between the goalposts that time."

Grant's eyes were round. "Was that the baby?"

"That's our little soccer star," Hunter said, giving his wife's shoulders one last brisk rub before lowering himself into the other wing chair. "She's been practicing on Raven's innards for a couple of months now."

"You called the baby 'she,'" Charli said with a smile, "and Raven called it 'he.' I thought nowadays everyone knew what they were having."

"They did ultrasound," Hunter said, "but we wouldn't let them tell us. We don't want to know ahead of time."

"And sometimes they're wrong," Raven said, stroking her stomach. "Anyway, we like surprises."

"Surprise!" Charli said. "I'm pregnant."

The women squealed in unison and rushed to hug Charli and Grant. The men gave Charli congratulatory kisses on the cheek; they pumped Grant's hand and thumped him on the back.

"We just found out," Grant said. He appeared both dazed and proud behind his wide grin.

"When are you due?" Raven asked.

"The beginning of August," Charli said. "Hottest part of the summer."

Sunny said, "At least you won't be stuck in the house with the baby. You can get out and go places."

Amanda was acutely conscious of Nick sitting close to her on the love seat. Their legs touched; his arm was thrown over her shoulders. She flicked him a glance, as if to say *Now's as good a time as any*. She'd warned him it would happen tonight.

She took a sip of espresso to wet her dry mouth—as if she needed the caffeine with her nerves already so wound up! "Nick and I have an announcement, too."

All eyes turned to her.

Under her white silk shantung blouse, her heart beat painfully. Why was it suddenly so hard to take this charade one step further? "Nick and I are getting married."

She sat there and let the wave of congratulations flow over her, the kisses, the heartfelt embraces, the I'm-so-happy-for-yous.

Amanda felt like a rat. Vaguely she was aware of Nick shaking hands, accepting the good wishes of her friends. Never had she found it so difficult to keep a smile on her face.

These were her dearest friends in the world, people she truly loved, and she was blatantly deceiving them, letting them think she'd found the kind of happily-ever-after they had. She hadn't thought about this when she'd devised her fake-boyfriend ruse to throw the Wedding Ring off the scent, hadn't thought about how low she'd feel doing this to them.

She reminded herself that if she hadn't taken drastic action, she wouldn't have had a moment's respite from their determined matchmaking. Not only that, she would have been prey to whatever devious scheme they'd cooked up. She was still convinced they'd been plotting something, and would have put it into action if she hadn't beaten them to the punch.

She told herself these things, but it did little to ease her conscience. She still felt like a rat.

Sunny said, "No ring?"

Amanda was ready for that. She was about to explain that she and Nick were going to go ring-hunting after the holidays when the shopping crowds died down, but he spoke up first.

"I thought Christmas Eve would be the appropriate time to present this," he said, reaching into the breast pocket of his sport coat.

Amanda's heartbeat went into double time, her smile pinned on like a mannequin's.

Damn it, I hate it when he does this!

What surprise did he have in store for her this time? If he'd bought her a ring...

But it wasn't a ring box he pulled out of his pocket. It was an ivory silk handkerchief, edged with lace. And decades old, by the looks of it. It was carefully wrapped around something.

Everyone was silent as he slowly peeled back the layers of silk. Amanda held her breath as he revealed a ring, obviously antique: a wide band of what appeared to be platinum in an open filigree design, set with diamonds. It was exquisite.

Amanda couldn't speak. She couldn't force sound from her throat as Nick lifted her left hand and slid the ring onto her finger.

She looked into his eyes and had the unnerving feeling that he was seeing straight through to her soul. His fingers tightened around hers, fractionally, before he released them.

Someone said, "I think she's speechless."

Everyone laughed. Amanda Coppersmith, at a loss for words?

"It belonged to my grandmother," Nick said.

"When she died, my folks gave it to me for my future bride."

Amanda looked down at her hand. The ring looked as if it had been made for her finger. Lifting her gaze once more, she shook her head helplessly. "Nick...this is a family heirloom. You can't give it to me!"

"This is getting to be a habit," Sunny said. "I've never known Amanda to turn down presents like she does with you, Nick. Does that mean it's true love?"

"We can hope so," he said, still holding Amanda's gaze. Quietly he said, "Grandma would have wanted you to have it. You remind me a lot of her. She had an opinion about everything, too." The others laughed again.

What kind of game are you playing? she silently asked him. *Why are you placing me in this impossible position?*

Her mind raced. She'd have to take very good care of this ring for however long their "engagement" lasted—another three weeks or so, the three-month mark, when she'd be officially free of her friends' romantic machinations. Then she could give him back the ring, along with a blistering piece of her mind, for putting her through all this.

His grandmother's ring! The man was certifiable!

During the past few weeks, since Nick had rescued her mother from that larcenous con man, he and Amanda had continued to go on "dates" at least twice a week, always with one or more Wedding Ring couple. But it was no longer the same. That incident with Liv had been a turning point of sorts, leaving Amanda jumpy and unsettled. How was she supposed to think of Nick simply as an employee, a beau-for-hire, after he'd performed such an incredibly personal service? He could have been hurt, for heaven's sake. He certainly would have been if that guy Connor had had his way.

The good news was that Mom and Dad had started talking. Amanda didn't know if anything would come of it, but it was a start. Meanwhile she'd taken Nick's advice and told Raven, Charli and Sunny about the separation. That hadn't been an easy conversation, but she was glad she'd finally had it. The strain of keeping everything hush-hush, hoping and praying for it all to blow over, had worn her down. And the secrecy was so unnecessary; as her friends had readily reminded her, they'd known her folks for as long as they'd known her. The unconditional love and support they'd shown Amanda and her parents had made her ashamed she'd waited so long to confide in them.

Kirk wore a devilish grin. "Aren't you forgetting something, Nick?"

"I haven't forgotten anything."

Amanda was trying to decipher the strange light in Nick's eye when he curled his hand around her neck and drew her to him. His mouth touched hers and immediately she knew this was not going to be like those other kisses, the chaste, dry pecks they'd shared for the benefit of their audience these past two and a half months.

His lips were warm and supple, and surprisingly soft as they caressed hers. He tasted of sweet zabaglione and bitter espresso. And, as the kiss deepened, he tasted of the man himself, mysterious and beguiling. Amanda knew they had to make it a good show, but that wasn't why she angled her head for greater contact; it wasn't why she leaned into him, just a little.

The fingers at her nape spread over her scalp, holding her. A little shudder ripped through her and she pressed fractionally closer, without meaning to. Had she ever been kissed like this?

When the tip of his tongue teased her lips, she opened for him without hesitation, felt the sleek, sensual probing in every part of her, from her sensitive mouth to her tingling breasts to the empty, aching depths of her belly.

At last he pulled away, slowly. The sense of loss was palpable, startling Amanda back to her senses. She blinked at Nick and saw a gentle smile tug at his mouth.

"Thank you for saying yes," he murmured.

She looked at the roomful of grinning people—and at Grandma Rossi, standing over her with a stern expression on her lined face.

"You marrying her?" Mrs. Rossi asked Nick.

"Yes, ma'am, I am," he proudly stated, holding Amanda's beringed left hand aloft as proof.

"Is okay, then." Mrs. Rossi shambled toward the wing chair occupied by Hunter. He sprang out of it and offered it to her.

Raven spoke up. "Have you set a date?"

Amanda sucked in a deep breath, struggling to organize her thoughts. "Um, no, we—"

"We were thinking mid-March," Nick said.

We were?

Charli, the Mistress of Organization, grabbed her purse from the floor and extracted her fat day planner. Flipping ahead in it, she said, "So we're talking the weekend of Saturday, March seventeenth. No, wait a minute. That's Saint Patrick's Day. How about the tenth?"

"Sounds good." Nick turned to Amanda. "Is the tenth all right with you?"

"Well, I...I'll have to check my calendar. We don't have to decide right this—"

"Is the tenth," Mrs. Rossi declared.

"Settled." Charli flipped to a pad of blank memo paper. "Who do you want to officiate?"

Amanda opened her mouth, but Nick cut her off. "I'd say my family priest, but I know Amanda isn't religious. I don't mind a justice of the peace."

Mrs. Rossi emitted a disparaging grunt.

"J.P. it is." Charli made a notation.

"I know someone," Grant offered. "I'll call him right after Christmas."

"Great," Nick said. "Thanks."

"Listen, uh..." Amanda felt like she was on some demented amusement-park ride that was stuck in high gear. "This is all premature."

"Are you kidding?" Sunny slid off Kirk's lap to sit on the floor between his knees. "With the wedding only two months off? You'll really have to hustle. That is, unless you just want to stroll into the county courthouse and get married there."

"Well, uh, that's an idea," Amanda ventured. "No muss, no fuss."

"Yeah, right." Nick crossed his ankle over his knee. He gave Amanda's shoulder an affectionate pat. "I only intend to get married once, and I'm going to do it right. Sorry, honey, we're having a real wedding."

All of a sudden she was "honey"?

"Where do you want to have it?" Raven asked. "It might be difficult booking a place on such short notice."

"You can have Stitches," Hunter offered. He and Raven had gotten married in his comedy club last April. "I'll reserve the date."

Nick turned to Amanda. "What do you think?"

She shook her head. "I don't even want to discuss—"

"You're right," Nick said. "Your house is the perfect location."

Did she say that?

"I agree." Charli tapped her chin with her mechanical pencil. "It'll be too cold for a tent wedding, but there's that enormous living room. And the kitchen's state of the art, so food prep will be no problem."

Nick asked, "What caterer would you suggest?"

Charli spread her hands. "Here I am."

"Oh, Charli, I can't let you do all that work. I'll hire someone," he protested.

"You don't know Charli like we do, Nick," Raven said with a smile. "She loves to cook for a crowd. And she's very good at it."

"Carlotta, she made me such a birthday party,"

Mrs. Rossi said in rhapsodic tones. "*Favoloso!* Eighty people, she cooked for."

"That was three years ago, when Nonni turned ninety," Charli said, and winked at her grandmother. "Wait till you see what I do when you turn a hundred."

"A hundred. Hah! I just want to live long enough to see this one married." She jerked her head toward Amanda, followed by a sharply wagging finger. "And no more *divorzi* for you!"

"Don't worry about that," Nick said. "Once this lady says 'I do,' I'll never let her go. I'm not like those other fools."

Charli was still fixated on the details. "Flowers."

Raven raised her hand. "I'll take care of it."

"Great." Charli made another mark in her book.

Amanda cried, "Don't order them yet!"

"Oh, I won't," Raven said, and Amanda breathed a sigh of relief, until Raven added, "I'll get a florist's book and bring it to you Tuesday evening. You can show me what you like and I'll order them Wednesday."

"And we'll settle on the menu then, too," Charli said. "No sense waiting till the last minute. We'll be at your place Tuesday at—" she glanced at Raven "—eight?"

"Eight's fine with me," Raven said.

"I won't be home then," Amanda lied. "I have an appointment."

"Cancel it." Charli turned to a clean page in her

book. "Now we need to talk about music, invitations and the guest list."

Nearly two hours later, Amanda was perilously close to confessing all—the phony-baloney boyfriend, the phony-baloney engagement—just to put the brakes on this runaway wedding train. Talk about things spinning out of control!

Charli closed her book with a snap. "I think that covers it for now. We all know what we have to do. Nick, don't forget to get those guest addresses."

He gave her a little salute. "I'll ask my mom for them tomorrow."

A voice from the living room entranceway said, "You know, I think we met before." It was Paul Rossi, one of Charli's five brothers, gesturing toward Nick with his beer bottle. Only Paul would be able to pack away a meal like that and drain a six-pack for dessert.

Nick said, "If you say so, but I don't recall it."

"Yeah, I know you," Paul said. "I thought I recognized you before, but I wasn't sure. You picked me up on Forty-fourth and Broadway a week or so ago. I was going to Penn."

Amanda's heart stopped beating for long, agonizing moments.

Paul sauntered into the room. "I remember you 'cause it was colder than a witch's tit—"

"*Paulo!*"

"Sorry, Nonni. Anyway, it was bitchin' cold that day—"

Mrs. Rossi threw up her hands, muttering something in Italian.

"—and I'd been pounding the pavement forever, trying to hail a cab," Paul continued, "and by the time I got in yours, my mouth wasn't working so good."

It's working just fine now, Amanda grumbled to herself, as the facade she'd so carefully constructed began to crumble around her.

Strangely, she felt something akin to relief, thinking that this whole disturbing business was about to come to an end. What had started out as an efficient solution to a specific problem has gotten so complicated that half the time she had to remind herself her relationship with Nick was a sham!

"My lips were frozen stiff," Paul said, "so when I told you 'Penn Station' it came out like—" He produced three unintelligible syllables, much to the amusement of his audience. "You can't understand me, you know? So I say it again, but it comes out even worse." He demonstrated, uttering the incomprehensible sounds more slowly and carefully.

Amanda felt Nick's body, pressed so close to her, shake with mirth. How could he laugh with everything falling apart like this?

"But you still don't get it," Paul said, "and now you're looking at me a little funny, so I'm getting a little desperate, you see. Last thing I need is to get booted out onto the street. So I make one last stab at it." Slower still, with painstaking care, he enunciated the garbled sounds. "That's when you turn to me with this real pitying look on your face and you say, 'Is there someone I can call to take care of you?'"

"That's some story," Nick chuckled, "but it wasn't me. Sorry."

"It *was* you!" Paul gestured emphatically with the beer bottle. "I looked right at you. I had to write out 'Penn Station' on a piece of scrap paper. We had us a little laugh about it, you and me."

Amanda watched Nick. He was the picture of serenity, maddeningly unruffled. She'd never known what an accomplished liar he was, a realization she found less than comforting.

"You know," Nick said, "a few months ago someone else told me there's this cabbie who looks just like me. Could be my twin, the guy said. I didn't think much of it at the time, but now?" He shrugged. "Who knows? Maybe we were separated at birth."

"He sounded just like you," Paul said.

"No kidding." Nick reached for his espresso cup.

Paul cogitated on this as he took a deep pull on the beer bottle. Amanda glanced around the room at her friends, all of whom appeared to be eating up Nick's separated-at-birth story. A frown tugged at her eyebrows. At the very least, she would have expected Sunny to jump on his lame explanation and have a little fun with it.

"Well, that's really something." Paul ambled out of the room, mumbling, "Coulda sworn it was the same guy."

Raven said, "Before we start exchanging Christmas presents, I think it only appropriate, under the circumstances, that we give Amanda and Nick their present first."

Their present? Amanda thought. As in a shared gift? She didn't like the sound of that.

"And isn't it just perfect after their announcement?" Sunny said.

"You're right," Charli agreed. "It's even better as an engagement gift."

"And better still—" Kirk nodded toward Mrs. Rossi, now snoring softly "—to present it while a certain party is blissfully unconscious."

"Well." Amanda's face ached with the strain of her forced smile. "Now you've got me intrigued."

Raven asked Hunter to retrieve an envelope from under the tree. He handed it to Amanda. Her name and Nick's were written on the outside in red and green ink.

"Whatever it is," she told Nick, "looks like we have to share."

"We'll be sharing everything else," he said with a smile. "May as well get used to it."

Opening the envelope, she pulled out a Christmas card with a cartoon image of Mommy kissing Santa under the tree. Inside she found a smaller gift-certificate envelope plus a handwritten note. She read it quickly.

"Oh no. You guys, this is... We can't accept this."

"What is it?" Nick took the note from her and read it. "Oh, wow."

"Of course you can accept it," Charli said.

"A gift certificate for a fancy dinner in Manhattan on New Year's Eve," Sunny said, "then you watch the ball go down in Times Square and stroll the short distance to the Marriott Marquis, where we've reserved a suite for you."

"A romantic New Year's with the man you love," Raven said. "What could be better?"

Never having come up with this cockamamie scheme in the first place, Amanda thought. *That would have been better.*

"This is an incredible gift," Nick said. "Thanks so much. We're going to have a blast. Aren't we, hon?" He patted Amanda's thigh.

Her mind rolled it around. The note said they'd have a suite. A suite meant more than one room. There was always a pull-out couch in the second room. She and Nick could toss a coin to see who got it.

"Yes, we are." She tried to sound sincere. "I've always wanted to see the ball come down. Thanks, guys."

9

"TEN!...Nine!...Eight!...Seven!..."

Nick put his arm around Amanda as the crowd in Times Square pressed around them on all sides, chanting the countdown to the New Year. His gesture was prompted by more than the bitter cold. About a half million people were packed into the renowned "Crossroads of the World," straining against police barricades, jostling the two of them, eliciting Nick's protective instincts.

"Six!...Five!...Four!..."

After a brief hesitation, Amanda slid her arm around his waist. He turned up the collar of her dark brown shearling coat, snugging it around her throat. Meanwhile the famous rhinestone-studded ball, six feet in diameter and brilliantly illuminated from within, made its way down the lofty flagpole atop One Times Square. The ball glowed like a sun against the night sky, drawing all eyes from the ever-present billboards, neon signs and humongous video monitors that made up the complexion of Times Square.

"Three!...Two!...One!...HAPPY NEW YEAR!"

As the ball reached the base of the flagpole, the numerals of the New Year lit up. The jubilant screams of the onlookers, the blare of horns and noisemakers, were practically deafening.

Nick pulled Amanda into his arms. She looked up at him, her eyes a bottomless silver lagoon beneath the glittering lights dancing on their surface. Their breath smoked in the cold, the puffs of vapor mingling between them. He put his mouth near her ear. "Happy New Year," he whispered, and kissed her.

She gave a little start, whether from the abrupt intimacy or the startling heat of it in this frigid weather, he couldn't say. She relaxed into his embrace then, her gloved fingers clinging to his overcoat while he let his lips tarry. Not as long as they had on Christmas Eve, when he'd had the pleasure of shocking her speechless, but long enough to drive home the fact that they were doing this not for the benefit of her watchful friends, but because *they* wanted to.

They separated. Amanda's eyes drifted open and locked on his. "Happy New Year," she said.

What should have been a short stroll to the nearby Marriott Marquis hotel took nearly twenty minutes as they wove their way through the teeming crowd, many of whom were speaking foreign languages. The New Year's Eve celebration in Times Square, close to a century-long tradition, attracted thousands of tourists, many from other countries. Here and there, mounted policemen helped to maintain order as the revelers began to disperse.

The evening had begun for Nick and Amanda with an exceptional meal at a Portuguese restaurant. They'd lingered over dessert, splitting most of a bottle of port, gearing up for the toe-numbing ordeal of standing outside for several hours in single-digit temperatures.

Having checked in to the hotel earlier, they proceeded directly to their suite. They didn't speak as they took one of the glass elevators to the twentieth floor. They didn't speak as they negotiated the long hallway.

Nick knew Amanda was nervous. In truth, he'd half expected her to decline this part of their shared gift, the "romantic" overnight stay in a hotel suite. Of course, her pals were sure to find out if she didn't spend the night here with him. That would look suspicious; they might begin to ask questions. Somehow, though, he sensed there was more to her presence here tonight than fear of seeing her clever scheme blow up in her face.

Or perhaps that was just wishful thinking on his part.

Nick produced his key card and let them into the suite. Lamps had been left on in the living room. His eyes immediately homed in on the round table in the corner and the items that had been deposited there, prettily arranged on a white tablecloth. A bottle of champagne in an ice bucket, two delicate champagne flutes and a platter of goodies.

"What's all that?" Amanda shed her coat, casting him a dubious glance. "Did you order it?"

Tossing his own coat on the sofa, Nick crossed to the table. "Me? Are you kidding? I'm a typical doltish male who'd never think of such a romantic gesture—"

he eyed her lovely, round bottom as she bent to pull off her black ankle boots ''—even if our engagement weren't of the pseudo variety. I detect a female hand at work here. Aha!'' he exclaimed, reading the small card that accompanied the spread.

"Don't tell me." She joined him at the table. "The Wedding Ring, right?"

He watched her realize what she'd said, watched her wish she could call back the words.

"There it is again," Nick said. "This mysterious reference to a Wedding Ring. Which I can now assume refers to our good pals Raven, Charli and Sunny. What is it, some sort of secret coven? Are you witches?" he teased.

"Maybe." She lifted a chocolate-dipped strawberry from the platter and bit into it. And let out an appreciative groan that bordered on the erotic.

"You, I could almost picture in a coven, with your apathy toward organized religion," he said, examining a smoked-salmon hors d'oeuvre. "But the other three attend church a little too regularly for me to buy the witch theory." He popped the hors d'oeuvre into his mouth. "Mm! This is *good!*"

Amanda faced him squarely. "We have to decide on sleeping arrangements."

"Of course, a significant hint might be the words '*Wedding Ring*.'" He flexed his fingers to insert quotation marks. "From which I can deduce that this group's mission statement might include words like *marriage*, *husband* and *china pattern*. Am I getting warm?"

"We should do this fairly," she said, digging in her change purse. "I'm not assuming I'm getting the bedroom just because I'm the woman. How can I not have any coins? I've usually got pennies coming out the wazoo!"

"Nonsense. You're too young to be going through your change."

"What?"

"Never mind. Bad joke. So the purpose of this Wedding Ring is what? Finding each other husbands? No, that's just too old-world. What is it really?"

"Do you have a coin?"

"Sure." Nick reached into his trouser pocket. "How much do you need? You're not gonna go looking for a soda machine, are you? There's a fully stocked fridge right over there, not to mention a whole bottle of bubbly. Speaking of which—"

"I'll toss you for it."

"The bubbly?"

"The *bedroom!*" She plucked a quarter from his open palm. "Heads I win—"

"Wait a minute. If you think I'm going to let a woman sleep on one of those lumpy pull-out contraptions when there's a real bed available, think again. We're not going to toss for the bedroom. It's yours."

"Don't be antediluvian. I intend to do this fairly."

"What would be fair is for you to let me be a gentleman and give you the bed."

Amanda prepared to toss the coin. "Heads I win."

"Have you ever just accepted something graciously?"

She flipped the quarter into the air and slapped it onto the back of her hand.

"We're going to let the coin decide," she decreed, and lifted her hand to reveal tails. She'd lost. Her eyebrows twitched together for an instant before she schooled her expression.

Nick said, "Don't say I didn't offer. Will you at least let me pull this thing out for you? The hotel must've figured we'd both be sleeping in the other room." He quickly hung up his overcoat, moved furniture out of the way, flung the cushions aside and unfolded the sofa into a bed. The mattress already sported fresh sheets and a blanket. He retrieved a pair of pillows from the closet and tossed them onto the bed with a flourish. "Ta da!"

"Huh. Thanks."

"What's wrong?"

"Nothing." Her gaze strayed through the open door of the bedroom, where a firm king-size bed waited, its covers turned down, two foil-wrapped chocolate mints on the pillows.

"This is what you wanted, right?" he pressed. "A fair coin toss."

"I said nothing's wrong!"

"Great. I always try to give a lady what she wants." Lifting the champagne bottle from the bucket of ice, he inspected the label and gave an appreciative whistle. "Piper Heidsieck. Someone's got good taste. Let's do this right. I'll pour us a couple of glasses while you change into something more comfortable."

The look on her face was priceless.

"Okay, let me clarify." He wrapped a cloth napkin around the head of the champagne bottle. "When I said 'something more comfortable,' I literally meant *something more comfortable.* Didn't you bring some flannel pj's? A fluffy robe or something?"

He watched her battle with indecision. That elegant pants outfit looked great on her, but it had been a long evening and she had to be ready to let her hair down. "I think I'll just go to bed," she said.

"Not until we've toasted the New Year." He twisted the bottle while keeping a firm grip on the cork. "I don't know what you're worried about. If I were the kind of guy who might attack you, it wouldn't much matter what you were wearing."

"If I thought you were the kind of guy who might attack me," she said, "I wouldn't be here with you now."

"See? We know each other better than you think." The cork came free with a soft pop. Nick filled the two flutes and set the bottle back in the ice bucket. He kicked off his shoes, tossed his suit jacket and necktie over a chair, loosened the collar and cuffs of his white dress shirt and pulled the tail out of his waistband. Throwing himself on the bed he'd just unfolded, he propped a pillow against the sofa back so he could sit with his legs extended. He grabbed the TV remote control and started channel-surfing. "Hurry up and change before the champagne goes flat."

Amanda disappeared into the bedroom, where they'd left their bags. Five minutes later she rejoined him, wearing a white, terry-lined silk jacquard robe over pale blue silk pajamas. She was barefoot. Her hair was loose, just grazing her shoulders.

Nick turned off the television. "Why don't you grab those glasses. And the bottle, too, while you're at it."

She placed the champagne on the lamp table next to Nick, and brought the platter of food as well, setting it on the blanket between them before shoving the other pillow behind her back as Nick had done, and sitting next to him on the sofa bed.

They clinked glasses. Amanda said, "Here's to a happy and prosperous New Year."

"May we both get what we most want." Nick took a sip. The champagne was cold and sparkly and delicious.

Neither spoke. It was a comfortable silence. Amanda perused the offerings on the platter and chose a marinated mushroom, while Nick worked his way through the smoked-salmon canapés.

"You know," she said at last, "I never did this with either of my husbands."

"Tossed a coin for the sofa bed?"

She made a face. "There were plenty of nights I would've liked to. No, I mean we never just sat quietly, enjoying each other's company."

"Never? That's hard to believe."

"There was always something going on, work or business trips, or one or both of us had some social obligation the other wanted no part of or..." She trailed off.

"Or?" he said.

Amanda looked at him for a long moment, as if

weighing a decision. She drained her glass and let him refill it. She didn't look at him as she finished, "Or he'd be slipping around with some other woman."

That hadn't been easy for her to admit, and Nick felt a surge of anger toward the bastard who'd hurt her. "Which one did that?"

"They both did. At least Roger knew how to be discreet. Ben's girlfriends used to call the house."

"Another mystery solved," he said.

"What do you mean?"

"I wondered why you left them."

Amanda speared another mushroom with her hors d'oeuvre pick. Her silence was telling.

"Were there other reasons?" he asked. As if infidelity weren't enough.

After a moment she said, "I'm really not comfortable talking about this."

"Amanda, look at me."

She did. She probably thought her carefully blank expression revealed nothing. If he were a casual observer, that might have been true. But Nick had learned to read Amanda Coppersmith pretty well during the past weeks. And right now he read a hurt that went deep.

Quietly he said, "I wish you'd trust me."

"I trust you, Nick. It's just...it's just no one else's business, that's all."

He brushed his knuckles down her satiny cheek. "It wasn't your fault, Amanda." She tried to avert her face; he didn't let her, his fingers firm on her jaw.

"Whatever made them such lousy husbands, it wasn't your fault. You didn't make it happen."

She jerked her head away. "How can you know that?"

Because no man in his right mind would step out on a lady like you. He didn't say it.

Amanda sat up straight. "Things aren't always what they seem. I wish people would stop making assumptions, stop—" She shook her head, as if to stem the tide of words.

But Nick had heard enough. He'd heard what she'd said and he'd heard the part she couldn't bring herself to say. So he said it for her. "You didn't leave Roger and Ben, did you, Amanda? They left you."

She sat hugging her knees to her chest, hiding her face under the fall of her hair. Nick wanted nothing more than to pull her into his embrace, to offer the comfort of his arms—but he knew she wasn't ready for that.

He was in no hurry. He refilled his glass, and hers. He ate a mozarella-and-tomato canapé and waited her out.

"I guess I can't blame everyone for thinking it was the other way around." Amanda's voice was hoarse. "It's this image I project—the one that says I don't need anybody, nothing gets to me. The Ice Queen in all her glory."

"No one who knows you thinks of you like that."

"Then why do they all just assume that I was the one who walked out—" Her voice broke, and Nick curled his hand into a fist to keep from reaching for her.

"How about because they all know how wonderful you are," he said, "and what losers your exes were?"

"That's easy to say, but outsiders can never know what goes on in a marriage. Not you, not my friends."

"That's true, but—"

"I screwed up, Nick." She faced him fully, let him see the anguish she no longer attempted to hide. "I failed. I wanted more than anything to be a good wife. I tried so hard, but I failed."

He frowned. "What does that mean, to be a good wife?"

She pushed her hair off her face, rubbed her damp eyes. "For starters? It means being woman enough to keep your man from wanting other women."

Nick couldn't help it; he laughed. "Honey, there's not much you can do to alter nature. Men are always going to want other women. No matter how much they love you."

Amanda blinked in astonishment, as if she'd assumed he was above so vile an impulse as infidelity. Nick found her faith in his character gratifying.

"Men always *want* it," he clarified. "It's what they do about it, or don't do about it, that counts. Your exes made their choice, and I'm betting they lived to regret it." Amanda started to object; he talked over her. "Yeah, yeah, I know, *they* left *you*. But let me ask you, weren't you getting a little fed up by then yourself?"

"Who wouldn't be?"

"And don't you think they picked up on that?"

She hesitated. "I suppose so."

"So did it ever occur to you that both Roger and Ben decided to beat you to the punch, rather than wait around for you to call a divorce attorney and serve them with papers?"

She started to shake her head, and he said, "Any guy with a serious ego, that's just the sort of thing he'd do. The last thing he'd want is to let his woman get the jump on him. Then he could spread it around what a lousy wife she was, how it was all her fault."

Amanda was giving this some thought, he could tell. She drank deeply from her champagne flute. Her eyes appeared slightly unfocused. She reached past him for the bottle and refilled her glass. Well, at least she'd sleep well tonight.

Could Amanda's disastrous marriages be at the root of her need to be in control? Nick wondered. If he'd been discarded by two wives in rapid succession, if his world and his dreams had been ripped apart not once but twice, he might feel a need to orchestrate every detail of his life, too, from business matters to personal relationships to projecting just the right public persona.

She flopped back against the pillow once more. A few drops of champagne spilled onto her robe, but she didn't seem to notice. "I know you're just trying to make me feel better," she said. "Maybe you even have a point, but it doesn't change the basic facts."

"Which are?"

"I'm no good at being a wife. I'm not cut out for it. Some people are. Some aren't. Once burned, twice shy, they say. Well, I've been burned twice, and that's enough to make me shy for life."

She studied the tiny bubbles in her champagne glass, and he studied her. "They were really bad, weren't they? The divorces?"

She took a sip. "The second one, last year, was the worst. There was a time when just forcing myself to get dressed and go to work was a monumental task. Every day I wondered if this was the day when I'd fall apart. When I'd curl up in a ball and give up on everything."

Nick turned on his side, leaning on an elbow. "But you were stronger than that."

She shrugged. "I got through it. Alone. It's not that Raven and Sunny and Charli didn't care—they did, very much so. But they just never knew what I was going through. I never let them see how bad it was for me."

"Why?"

"I was afraid that if I let myself talk about it, if I relaxed this rigid control I had on my feelings, I'd...just come apart. I'd never be whole again." She glanced at him. "I don't expect you to understand."

He brushed strands of fine blond hair off her forehead. "I think I do." There it was again, the issue of control. "Did you ever get counseling?"

She made a wry face. "I should have, I guess. But like I said, I just couldn't talk about it. And I was kind of in denial, too. I told myself it's not that bad, I can handle this on my own, I've been through it before."

"And not so long before, right?"

She nodded. "My divorce from Roger was finalized three years ago this month. I met Ben on the rebound. He seemed so fun-loving, so candid and sincere. Refreshingly different from Roger. Or so I thought. In the ways that counted, they were cut from the same cloth." She lifted another strawberry from the platter, this one coated in white chocolate, and nibbled at it.

No wonder she was so skittish about relationships, Nick thought. With a history like that, chances were she no longer trusted her choice in men.

Amanda looked slumberous and sensual, sprawled against the pillow with in her pj's and robe, her face flushed from the champagne, her hair slightly mussed. Nick felt himself respond physically, so he resorted to his little trick to distract himself. He selected two distant locations in the city and began mentally calculating the most efficient driving route between them.

Let's see. Times Square to La Guardia Airport. Head east on Fortieth to the FDR Drive...

Amanda focused her groggy gaze on him. "Now it's your turn."

"To do what?"

"To come clean like I did."

"About what? I've never been divorced. Or even married, for that matter."

She pointed an elegantly manicured finger at him. "That's it on the button. Don't you remember that night after my birthday party, when you said if I told you about my divorces, you'd tell me why you never got married?"

"The way I remember it, I said that if you told me why you married those two losers—not why you divorced them—I'd spill my guts. So you still owe me an answer."

"Why does anyone tie the knot with the wrong person?" Throwing her arms over her head, she stretched languorously.

Nick discreetly adjusted his shirttail, thankful it was a long one. *Take the FDR Drive north to the Triborough Bridge...*

Down, boy.

"I'm not letting you get away with that," he said. "What did your exes have in common? Somehow Roger and Ben must have both touched you in the same way."

Amanda started to giggle just as the champagne glass touched her lips, resulting in yet more wine soaking into her robe. "That's just it. They both touched me in the same way, all right." Nick was about to ask what that meant when she added, "I have this unfortunate habit of marrying any man I sleep with." She slapped a hand over her mouth, obviously regretting the tipsy revelation.

"So what you're saying is, Roger and Ben are the only men you've had sex with."

She scowled. "What made me say that?"

Can't imagine, he thought as she reached across him again for the champagne bottle.

"You might want to take it easy with that stuff," he advised. "You're gonna feel like death warmed over in the morning."

"Okay, now you know the shameful truth." She poured herself another glass. "I'm practically a virgin."

"Well, I wouldn't say—"

"So fess up. How come you never married?"

"I almost did, once."

"What happened?" she asked.

"She tried to change me. I didn't like it. So I called it quits."

"Just like that?"

"Nothing is ever 'just like that,'" he said, "but yeah, that's the gist of it."

Amanda cocked her head. "What did she try to change about you?"

"The same thing my parents tried to change. What I did for a living."

"Oh. Well, maybe they just recognized your potential, wanted something better for you."

"Samantha wanted something better for *herself*, if you ask me. Though I have to admit, it must've been a shocker for all of them when I quit my job to become a cabbie and part-time carpenter."

"What kind of job did you have?"

"I was a fund manager for Paragon Investments," Nick said.

Amanda's jaw dropped. "You're kidding!"

"Is it so hard to believe?"

She stared at him. "No. No, it isn't. I'm sorry, I'm just...surprised. Oh, God..." she groaned, cradling her forehead in her hand.

"What?"

"What I said to you, during that ride home after my birthday party. Remember? I said I couldn't tell people you were a financial analyst. I said what if someone asked you about it and discovered you can't discuss the subject."

"Actually, the term you used was 'converse intelligently.'" He smiled, remembering. "You expressed doubts about my ability to pass myself off as a financial analyst or a neurosurgeon. If it makes you feel any better, I'm dumb as a stump when it comes to brain surgery."

"I must've sounded so..."

"Don't worry about it. How were you to know what I did in a previous incarnation?"

"But that's just it. I didn't know. I assumed. I never even asked you about yourself."

"You asked what I wear under my breeches."

She sent him a sidelong smirk. "That doesn't count."

Are you still curious? He bit his tongue to keep from asking it.

"So you obviously went to college," she said.

He nodded. "I have a degree from Carnegie Mellon."

Her eyes grew round. "And you threw all that away?"

"I don't feel like I threw anything away. I worked in the investment field for seven long years. I can't tell you how frustrated I was in that environment. It wasn't for me—the hustling, the back stabbing, being cooped up in an office all day. Finally I admitted to myself that I'm just not suited to the corporate grind."

"So you started driving a cab."

"It was supposed to be a temporary thing," he said. "I found out I liked it."

"And you've never looked back."

"I've never looked back."

After a moment she said, "I guess that takes a kind of courage, trusting your instincts enough to make such a drastic change in your life."

"I don't know about courage, but I'm a lot more content than I was then. My income may not be what it was, but the money's steady enough and I'm not eating cat food."

"So you have everything you need."

"Everything I need, perhaps. Not everything I want."

"Does anyone ever have everything they want? I *want* to see a subscription to *Grasshopper* in every English-speaking home where there's a child under ten. But I'm a realist. I know that's not going to happen in my lifetime."

"What about in your personal life?" he asked. "What do you want most of all?"

"That's easy. I want my well-meaning pals to stop trying to set me up with Mr. Right."

"Maybe they just hate seeing you lonely."

"Who says I'm lonely? I have friends, relatives, a business that keeps me hopping." Responding to his dubious expression, she shot back, "So let me ask you—are *you* lonely?"

"As a matter of fact, I am." The admission surprised her, he could tell. "I don't think I was meant to live alone."

She said, "And yet you've chosen not to marry."

"I've chosen not to marry the wrong person."

"Ah." She touched her chest. "My particular specialty."

They polished off the hors d'oeuvres in silence. Nick got up and carried the empty platter, bottle and glasses to the table. Amanda's heavy-eyed gaze tracked his movements. He leaned over her, bracing his arms on either side of her.

"Happy New Year again," he murmured, and pressed a kiss to her forehead. Their eyes met and something arced between them. When their lips touched, he couldn't say who initiated it, but it no longer mattered. The energy flowed both ways, feeding on itself. And still the only point of contact was their mouths.

That changed. Amanda's arms snaked around his neck, pulling him to her, and he didn't fight it. He was helpless to fight it. He'd wanted this woman since the day he'd first set eyes on her. He joined her on the bed, half lying on her, their limbs tangled. The kiss went on seemingly without end, deep and hungry, as if they'd waited nearly three months for just this moment.

Nick lifted his head at last and stared down at Amanda. His gaze traveled from her slumberous eyes to her rosy cheeks to her mouth, now damp and parted and slightly swollen. He felt himself tugged in two directions. Amanda's hand slid under his loose shirttail and over his bare back, nudging his will in the direction of his heart rather than his head.

He kissed her throat, that tender patch of skin where her neck curved into her shoulder, the very spot he'd had his eye on for so long, wondering how it tasted. It tasted like Amanda always smelled, warm and womanly and mysterious. She arched against him with a soft gasp, clinging to him. She had to feel his erection, pressing against her hip.

He felt her mounting excitement as she pushed his shirt up, as her hands roamed from his back to his chest, touching, stroking. Nick struggled to restrain himself, but it was a losing battle. She filled his senses—her supple heat under his hands, the scent of her in his nostrils, the lingering taste of her on his lips—until all he could think about was feeding his hunger for her.

He tore at the tie of her robe and spread it open. Her chest rose and fell in a heightened rhythm, the nipples of her small breasts jutting against the thin silk of her pajamas. Nick felt reason desert him as he lowered his mouth to one erect peak. Amanda cried out, bucking beneath him, her fingernails digging into his shoulders under his rucked-up shirt.

He suckled her, drawing on her hard, scraping her lightly with his teeth, licking her with firm strokes through the wet silk. The desperate, breathy sounds she made tested the limits of his control. Too impatient for buttons, he pushed her pajama top up to her shoulders. A dark flush of arousal stained her chest.

She moved restlessly against him, an invitation impossible to resist.

Nick kissed her panting mouth before moving lower to press openmouthed kisses to her perfect, gently rounded breasts, to the rosy tips, now tightly puckered. Amanda moved her head from side to side; he let her whimpers of pleasure guide him.

When at last he raised his head, she yanked his shirt up and off of him, leaving his torso bare. She slid her hands down his back to his buttocks and pulled him hard against her, kissing him hungrily.

Dangerously close to stripping off her pajama bottoms and plunging into her right then and there, Nick forced himself to pull back, trembling with the effort. He forced himself to say, "Amanda, honey, we have to stop."

"No, we don't."

"Yes." He kissed her lightly, pulling down her pajama top to cover her. "We do." He started to rise. She stopped him.

"Nick." Amanda smiled up at him, a candid smile that held nothing back, not her need, sharp and sweet, nor her heady sense of anticipation. She revealed it all, trusting him. "I want you. I want to make love with you."

She tried to kiss him. Gently he touched her lips, thwarting her. With a teasing smile he said, "Aren't you the lady with the unfortunate habit of marrying any man she sleeps with?"

"Is that what you're worried about? Never fear. I've

decided to eliminate all my bad habits, starting with that one."

"That's not what I'm worried about." Nick couldn't make his brain function when he was lying entwined with her; he moved to sit on the edge of the bed. "I want to make love with you, too, but it's not a good idea. Not right now."

A wary watchfulness had dimmed her smile. "Sure feels like it is."

"You won't think so in the morning."

"You don't think I know my own mind?"

"Amanda. You've had a lot of champagne, honey. You're going to feel miserable enough tomorrow without having something like this to regret."

"It's not the champagne making me want to..." Her words trailed off. His expression must have told her it wasn't going to happen. Embarrassed color suffused her face. She sat up and drew the sides of her robe together.

Nick knew he'd hurt her, and he hated himself for it. He should never have allowed things to get this out of hand. The last thing he wanted was to contribute to her feelings of rejection and abandonment, after what her ex-husbands had put her through.

But he'd never taken advantage of an inebriated woman, and he wasn't about to start now. Not with this of all women. Amanda hadn't been with a man for well over a year, since sometime before her divorce from Ben. She wasn't just tipsy, she was emotionally vulnerable. If they made love now, Nick had no doubt she'd regret it. She'd regret it and she'd withdraw from him, and that would be counterproductive to his overriding goal.

He lifted her hand and softly kissed her knuckles. His grandmother's platinum-and-diamond ring glittered on her finger. "Amanda—"

She jerked her hand away and tied the sash on her robe. She didn't look at him. "Good night, Nick."

"This is my fault," he said. She didn't respond. Rising, he picked up his shirt from the foot of the bed where she'd flung it. "We'll talk about this in the morning." He let himself into the bedroom and closed the door behind him.

10

THEY DIDN'T TALK ABOUT IT in the morning. Nick tried to, but Amanda stonewalled him. She knew there was nothing to talk about.

"I want you," she'd pleaded, as she'd practically torn his clothes off. "I want to make love with you." And he'd claimed to want her, too, lying like the gentleman he was, right before he peeled her off of himself and hightailed it out of there.

Even now, five days later, as she headed for the exit at Saks Fifth Avenue with her bulging shopping bag, Amanda felt a scalding rush of shame. Not for the first time, she wished she'd drunk enough that night to forget what a monumental fool she'd made of herself. She'd certainly drunk enough to produce a hellish hangover the next morning. Nick had been right about that.

He'd been right, too, about sex with him being a bad idea. She knew that now. She also knew it wasn't the champagne that had made her want him so desperately on New Year's Eve. But if he ever pressed her, she'd swear it had been precisely that, the alcohol going to her head.

Meanwhile she'd managed to avoid that promised conversation for five days. With any luck, they'd

never have it. After all, their "relationship" only
needed to last another six days. January 11 would
mark three months from the date she'd first started
seeing Nick. Under the renegotiated terms of the
Wedding Ring pact, as long as she became engaged
and the two of them had been dating for three months,
she could call it quits anytime after that and be off the
hook forevermore as far as Wedding Ring matchmaking attempts were concerned.

She'd give it at least a week after the eleventh,
maybe two, so the timing wouldn't look too suspicious, then she'd make the announcement: *Thanks for
all your unsolicited help, guys, but the wedding's off.*

If the thought of being free of Nick in the next couple of weeks didn't make her feel all warm and fuzzy,
that was only because she'd gotten used to having him
around. Maybe they could remain friends, she
thought. Maybe she and Nick could get together for
dinner once in a while, just to chew the fat, without the
Wedding Ring crew breathing down their necks.

It was lunchtime and the street-level selling floor of
Saks was choked with customers. Amanda wove
through them with the ease and skill of the power
shopper she was, past glass counters and merchandise
displays, her eye on the revolving doors.

"Amanda!"

She turned and spied Ben making a beeline for her
from the direction of the men's department. No fewer
than four shopping bags dangled from his fingers.
When it came to power-shopping, her second ex-
husband put her to shame.

Ben liked things. Expensive things. And as the chief executive officer of a Fortune 500 sporting goods company, he could afford them—up to a point. It hadn't taken long for his spendthrift ways to undermine the stability of their marriage. But by then his womanizing had taken its toll, so there wasn't all that much left to undermine.

Watching Ben approach her now, with his gleaming bleached grin and out-of-season tan, she couldn't help but wonder how close Nick had come to the truth when he'd suggested that her exes had dumped her primarily to avoid becoming the dumpees themselves. "Any guy with a serious ego," Nick had said, "that's just the sort of thing he'd do."

If there was anything Ben excelled at more than spending money, it was feeding his voracious ego. Roger, likewise, was no slouch in that area.

What did it say about her that she'd chosen men like that for the ultimate till-death-do-you-part commitment?

You sure can pick 'em, girl.

When Ben reached her, he went for the full-mouth kiss, but she turned her cheek and it landed near her ear.

"You're looking great, Amanda."

"Thanks. You, too." She didn't want to stare too openly, but she'd have sworn last time she saw him, Ben's temples had begun to sport a little gray. Now, however, his hair was a uniform light brown. It was a good dye job, and no doubt an expensive one. "You look youthful," she added.

"You think so?" Ben steered her out of the stream of lunchtime shoppers to a relatively quiet pocket of space in the women's belt department. They set down their shopping bags. "I've been working out. Does it show?" His buttery, black leather coat was open, and he reached inside it to thump his flat abdomen.

"Sure." Ben had no idea what she'd gone through when their marriage broke up, Amanda realized. Not an inkling about the depression that had threatened to swallow her whole. For his part, he'd been unconvincingly distraught over the divorce and had assuaged his grief with a brand-new thirty-foot cabin cruiser. He'd named it after his baby-faced slut du jour: the *Ashley*.

Amanda asked, "How's business?" knowing what his automatic answer would be.

"Incredible! Couldn't be better." Ben believed that to be successful, one had to show the world a positive face, twenty-four seven. The truth could be either extreme or somewhere in the middle.

Amanda was beginning to perspire under her heavy shearling coat. "That's great. Listen, I've got to get back to the—"

"I hear you're seeing someone. Is it serious?"

She wasn't surprised. Word traveled. Plus, Ben's interest in her had experienced a dramatic revival once they were no longer married.

"It's serious enough," she said, hoping he'd leave it at that.

"What's his name?"

"Nick Stephanos."

"What does he do?"

The all-important question. With this crucial nugget of information, Ben would be able to fit Nick into the appropriate socioeconomic slot. He'd be able to gauge Nick's success quotient and compare it to his own.

Amanda almost said, *He drives a cab and he's twice the man you are.*

The instant she thought it, she knew it was true.

"He owns a fleet of limos," Amanda said, knowing she had to stick to the story she'd concocted, no matter how entertaining it would have been to tell the truth and watch her ex-husband's face.

"Huh. A big fleet?" he asked.

"The biggest. He's expanded nationwide and has satellite locations in Hong Kong, London, Frankfurt and Tokyo."

"Huh! Well. Looks like you did okay for yourself."

"By the way, *Grasshopper's* doing great, steadily building market share. Thanks for asking."

Ben pulled a face. It had been a bone of contention between them that he never took her business seriously.

"We're getting married," Amanda blurted, and had the satisfaction of seeing his eyes bug out in astonishment.

"You're kidding! Really?"

Well, no, not really, but that didn't stop her from holding up her left hand and wiggling her ring finger. "Nice, huh? It was Nick's grandmother's. A family heirloom."

"How long have you known this guy?" he demanded.

"Long enough to know it's the real thing."

"Yeah, well, you thought that before."

Amanda's fingernails itched to claw that smug grin off his face. "What can I tell you? It took a couple of mistakes to show me what true love really is."

Ben didn't like being called a mistake. A muscle near his eye twitched. "Well, look before you leap— that's all I can say. I don't want to see you hurt."

A sentiment that struck Amanda as hypocritical in the extreme, considering Ben had hurt her worse than anyone else ever had.

"You know..." He gave her his smoothest smile. "I always thought you and I could've made it work. Sometimes I still think that."

"The operative word in 'make it work' is *work*, Ben. Two people have to make the effort."

He moved a little closer. "I miss you, Amanda. I'm not ashamed to admit that."

"That's interesting. What does shame you? Certainly not having motel sex with your manicurist while I waited at home with your birthday dinner growing cold on the table. Or racking up an astronomical debt at Atlantic City and nearly bankrupting us. That didn't seem to cause much shame, either."

"I'll tell you why I left you," he growled, with an ugly sneer. "You don't know how to make a man feel like a man. Never could cut me any slack. If you hadn't been so damn judgmental, if you'd given me just a little understanding and support like a wife should, I never would've looked twice at that manicurist, or any of the others."

A year ago, this diatribe would have devastated Amanda, reinforcing her conviction that she was a failure as a wife. Now, all she heard was the spiteful rantings of a shallow, self-important clod. Ben no longer had the power to hurt her, and the realization made her feel light as air.

Amanda said, "I'd love to stand around here and discuss how your weaknesses are my fault, but I have a business to run." She picked up her shopping bag. "Goodbye, Ben."

"I WAS EXPECTING MORE, after all the hype," Kirk said the next evening as he steered his new Maxima through the dark back roads of Amanda's neighborhood.

"Me, too." Amanda spoke up from the back seat. "The reviewers must've been on drugs." They were talking about the latest Liam Neeson film, a historical action picture, which she'd just seen with Nick, Sunny and Kirk. Now they were on their way to her house for dessert and coffee.

"The battle scenes were amazing," Nick offered, to the murmured agreement of the others. "I can't say that about the story, though, or the writing or the casting."

"Except for Liam." Sunny, sitting in the front passenger seat, addressed Amanda and Nick over her shoulder. "I'll gladly pay money to see anything he's in."

"Aha!" Kirk said with a grin. "I was wondering why you gave in so graciously and didn't lobby for another chick flick."

He pulled into Amanda's driveway and cut the engine in front of the two-car garage. They piled out of the car and followed the brick walkway to the front porch. The house looked warm and welcoming, with the porch light on and the first-floor windows glowing. Amanda hated coming home to a deserted-looking house. She loved the big, modern stone-and-cedar structure, but the fact was it was just too much house for one person.

Unlocking the front door, she stepped through the foyer to the living room, with the others on her heels. "Should I make decaf or reg—"

"*SURPRISE!*"

Amanda's heart flipped over as dozens of people sprang from behind her furniture and poured through doorways. Sunny and Kirk stood laughing, along with everyone else, at her poleaxed expression.

Everyone Amanda had ever met had just materialized in her living room! All of her friends appeared to be there, as well as most of the staff of *Grasshopper* and every relative who lived within a day's drive.

There was Amanda's dad, holding hands with her beaming mother, who'd moved back in with him just two days earlier. Jared and Noelle were present, as were Amanda's grandparents, who'd traveled all the way from Maryland.

She saw a whole bunch of people she didn't recognize, now assaulting Nick with bear hugs, kisses and hearty back-slaps.

Nick's friends? Yes, it had to be. His friends and, by the looks of it, his relatives, too.

Oh no, Amanda thought. *They didn't!*

"We knew you'd never agree to an engagement party if we asked you," Raven told her, "so *surprise!*"

They did.

Stunned, Amanda let herself be dragged into the festivities, which had apparently been going on for some time before their arrival. She had a polite smile for Nick's parents when he introduced them. George Stephanos was an older and still handsome version of his son. His wife, Eunice, was an attractive, soft-spoken woman who obviously took good care of herself.

Amanda met Nick's younger sister and brother, Candace and Peter, and their spouses. Candace had recently completed her medical residency and had joined a pediatric practice in Queens. Peter was a staff reporter for the *New York Times*. They both had children, now home with baby-sitters.

Amanda struggled to maintain her smile as these warm, sincere people congratulated her and welcomed her into the Stephanos family. Eunice's eyes filled with happy tears as she held Amanda's hand and exclaimed over how well her mother's ring fit Amanda's finger. "And someday you'll pass it on to another generation." Overcome by emotion, she gave her future daughter-in-law a heartfelt hug. "I can tell already, my Nikolaos has found himself a special woman."

Amanda cast Nick a helpless look over his mother's shoulder. His enigmatic gaze gave nothing away, but she had the unsettling feeling that this party wasn't a surprise for him.

But that wasn't possible. If he'd had an inkling beforehand, he'd have warned her. He'd have warned her and she'd have taken steps to nip it in the bud.

Oh Lord, what if one of my friends says something to Nick's family about him owning a fleet of limos?

Someone pressed a drink into Amanda's hands. Blindly she gulped half of it down, praying that it was something strong. It looked like sparkling Pellegrino water, her usual choice, but blessedly it turned out to be a stiff vodka tonic.

The throng parted for an instant and she spied the glass-topped console table on the far end of her enormous living room, now piled high with wrapped boxes.

Engagement presents! What on earth was she going to do with those?

"Nick, this is lunacy!" Amanda hissed into his ear. "All these people think we're getting married!"

"Wasn't that the idea?"

"The idea was to fool a handful of my closest friends, not half the free world. Good grief, is that my dentist?"

Nick's hand slid around her waist. He leaned in close, his breath warm against her cheek. "Smile, Amanda. People are watching you."

"This has gotten out of hand. I can't do this anymore."

"Sure you can." He was maddeningly unperturbed. "Just relax and enjoy the party. But don't enjoy it too much," he added, tapping a finger against the glass she was rapidly draining. "Remember how you felt the morning after that New Year's champagne."

"It's all your doing," she groused. "I was practically a teetotaler before I met you."

Nick laughed. "Don't blame your bad habits on me," he said, reminding Amanda of her conversation yesterday with Ben.

That had been satisfying, putting her ex-husband in his place after all he'd put her through. Ben had stood gaping in shock as she'd turned her back and sailed out of the store. Her employees hadn't known what to make of the self-satisfied smile she wore for the rest of the day.

Amanda endured the remainder of the party in a mental fog, despite switching from vodka to mineral water after the first drink. Her friends and family besieged her with questions: had she ordered a wedding gown yet? What did it look like? Where would they honeymoon? Would Nick be moving into her house or were they planning to buy a new place? And a hundred other innocent queries that had forced Amanda to do some quick thinking, when thinking was the last thing she felt capable of in her present state of mind.

At one point she found herself alone with her brother in the kitchen. "I wish you'd warned me about this," she grumbled.

"That's the thing about surprise parties." Jared hauled a ten-pound bag of ice from the freezer and started transferring some of it to an ice bucket. "You don't get any warning."

"Well, this whole thing is very...awkward for me."

"Why? Your friends just want to celebrate your happiness. What's wrong with that?"

Amanda had a sudden urge to tell him precisely what was wrong with that, to blurt it all out, to unburden herself to her brother. Her conscience gave her no mercy. All these people, here for her, happy for her, wishing her all the joy and fulfillment that life had to offer, *giving her engagement presents, for heaven's sake!* What would they think if they knew how she'd deceived them? What would Nick's *parents* think? They seemed like such sweet, good-hearted people. She couldn't stand the thought of disappointing them when their son's "engagement" fell through.

She curled her left hand at her side so she wouldn't have to see the ring.

Some ice cubes fell to the terra-cotta floor. Amanda squatted to pick them up and toss them in the sink. Jared thanked her. She leaned against the central cooking island, watching him tie the ice bag closed and return it to the freezer. "Jared...has Raven or Charli or Sunny ever asked you to, uh, participate in any kind of funny business?"

"In my dreams. But that's all in the past. I'm an old married man now," he said with a wink. "I don't have dreams like those anymore."

According to Nick, all men had dreams like those.

Some chose to act on them, and some chose to honor their marriage vows. She could have told him a lot of women had dreams like those, too.

"I didn't mean that kind of funny business," she said. "I meant...well, did they ever ask you to participate in any kind of, um, subterfuge? That, you know, had to do with me?"

"Yeah, as a matter of fact, they did."

Amanda swallowed a gasp. She straightened from the counter. "They did? What did they ask you to do?"

"They asked me not to tell you they were planning a surprise engagement party."

She snatched a handful of ice cubes from the sink and tried to shove them down his shirt, but he was too nimble for her. "You know I don't mean that!" she said.

"Well then, what do you mean? 'Subterfuge.' Sounds real cloak-and-dagger."

Amanda sighed in exasperation. "Did they try to fool me, is what I mean."

"Fool you how?"

She wished she could ask him directly about her suspicions back in October when she'd accused her Wedding Ring pals of enlisting her brother's aid in whatever devious matchmaking plan they'd concocted. She still didn't know what they'd had up their sleeves back then, only that she'd managed to thwart it by implementing her own devious plan first.

She couldn't be more specific in her questioning of Jared without revealing the details of the Wedding

Ring pact. And that she refused to do. It was a confidential agreement, a sacred vow between best friends, even if her current mature wisdom revealed it as nothing more than a silly adolescent whim. She simply couldn't violate her friends' trust by letting anyone else in on it.

But she could violate their trust by pretending to have found her happily-ever-after mate.

Having no desire to explore that particular train of thought, she gave herself a mental shake and said, "It's not important. I just thought they might've asked you to help them...play a trick on me."

"A practical joke, you mean."

"Something like that. Forget I said anything."

Only much later, when almost all the guests had departed, did Amanda discover her parents had packed an overnight bag. That wasn't unusual. They'd moved to the southern part of New Jersey several years earlier, and often stayed in one of their daughter's spare rooms rather than make the long drive home at night.

"Grandma and Grandpa came in from Maryland with Barb and Hal," Liv said, naming Amanda's first cousin and her husband, who also lived near Baltimore. "They're all planning to stay over, too. I hope that's all right."

"Well, of course it is." Amanda had four bedrooms; it would be a full house. In the morning she'd take everyone to Wafflemania, the local diner where Sunny had waitressed for a dozen years before marrying Kirk.

"Now, don't you bother with us," Liv said. "We

know where the sheets and towels are, and we'll make sure the others are comfortable. You and Nick won't even know we're here."

"Nick? Oh, he's not staying here."

Sunny's voice behind Amanda made her jump. "Since when? You two were making breakfast plans earlier."

Amanda would have liked to dispute that, but the fact was she and Nick had deliberately led Sunny and the others to believe that he spent many nights at her house, as a real fiancé would. Earlier in the evening Amanda had indeed asked Nick, in Sunny and Kirk's presence, where he wanted to go for breakfast tomorrow. It was all part of the act, an act she was coming to despise more and more by the minute.

"Well, I don't, um...I mean, Nick doesn't really have to..." Amanda glared at her "fiancé" mutely pleading with him to jump into the conversation. When he chose not to do so, she declared, "Nick will sleep on the sofa."

"He'll have to fight me for it," Grandpa said, dropping heavily onto the couch as if to claim squatter's rights. He bounced a couple of times to test the springs. "I can't take Myrtle's snoring. I'm sleeping here."

Amanda's grandmother said, "Suit yourself, you old grump."

"Listen, princess." Amanda's father put his arm around her shoulders. "I don't know who you're trying to kid, playing coy like this, but none of us were born yesterday. You're a thirty-year-old, two-time divorcée, engaged to be married, and this is your own home."

Grandpa gestured broadly. "Shack up with whoever you want, girl. We're all free-thinkers around here."

"Off to bed with you two." Grandma shooed Amanda and Nick up the stairs. "We'll see you in the a.m."

11

"DON'T ASK ME for a coin," Nick said, both amused and intrigued by this turn of events. "I'm not tossing you for the bed."

They stood in Amanda's bedroom, on either side of her queen-size bed, which was draped in a silky, pale yellow and ivory striped comforter.

"It's as if the whole world is conspiring to throw us into bed together!" she snapped. "First that hotel suite, now this! It's almost as if they all know what we've been up to."

"It might be a good idea to keep our voices down."

"There's nowhere to sleep in here but the bed," she fretted. "Except the floor. Maybe if I put a thick comforter on the carpet, I can make a kind of sleeping pallet...."

"You're going to make me sleep on the floor?"

"No, I will."

"Not this again. Amanda, neither one of us is going to sleep on the floor when there's a bed right here that's plenty big enough for two." She started to shake her head, and he added dryly, "I think I can manage to control myself."

"Yes, I'm sure you can."

He frowned. *What was that about?* "Listen, we don't

seem to have much choice about sleeping arrangements." He pulled off his cream-colored fisherman's sweater and tossed it on the chair in front of her dressing table. "I'm going to bed."

She eyed him suspiciously. "You don't have any pajamas here."

Nick grinned. "This is where you finally get to see what I wear under my breeches." He stripped off his undershirt, shoes and socks, and unbuckled the belt holding up his khaki slacks. Amanda seemed not to know where to look. Silly of her to be embarrassed, considering all that had transpired between them on New Year's Eve. He dropped his pants and laid them on the chair over his sweater, then held his arms out from his sides, inviting her to look her fill.

She did, at last. A small smile crept onto her face. "I was wrong."

"You said white briefs." He snapped the elastic waistband of his plaid boxer shorts. "Your turn. I'm guessing a silk satin bra and a pair of those little bikini panties cut high on the legs. Maybe even a thong."

Her smile was lopsided as she scooped a pair of pj's—pale pink silk this time—out of a drawer and headed for the adjoining master bathroom. "I'll let you keep guessing."

After Amanda was finished in the bathroom, Nick washed up. When he came out, she was already in bed, lying on her back near one edge of it. The table lamp on the other side was lit, and he turned it off as he slid between the cool sheets next to her. No parts of their bodies touched, yet he sensed her tension. They lay quietly in the dark, listening to Amanda's house-guests get settled for the night. Finally all was quiet.

Nick couldn't see her, but his other senses compensated. If he listened carefully, he could hear her soft inhalations. Her warmth crept to his side of the bed, bringing with it the intoxicating scent of her, reminding him of New Year's Eve and another bed. Too vividly he recalled the feel of her under his hands, the taste of her, the way she'd moved against him, with an artless passion that belied her self-appointed label of Ice Queen. He recalled, too, the monumental effort it had taken to stop, to get up and walk out of the room.

And he recalled her hurt and embarrassment when he had. Nick turned his head, squinting in the dark, trying without success to make out her profile. They'd never talked about that. Each time he'd brought it up, she'd put him off.

"Amanda." His voice was low, practically a whisper. He sensed her turning toward him. "What did you mean before, when you said you were sure I could control myself sharing a bed with you?"

After a moment she said, "I didn't mean anything. Except that you were only stating the obvious."

Nick shifted onto his side, leaning up on an elbow. "Do you think it's easy?"

Her harsh sigh told him she didn't want to discuss it.

Too bad. "Answer me, Amanda."

"I'm tired, Nick. Good night."

The truth struck him with the force of a wrecking

ball. "You think I didn't really want to make love with you on New Year's."

"There's no need to belabor this."

"How can you doubt how much I wanted you? Wasn't it obvious—"

"You restrained yourself easily enough," she snapped. The covers moved, and Nick knew she was throwing her arms over her eyes, as if to block out the unpleasant memories.

He couldn't hold back a wry chuckle. "I know that you know how turned on I was. We were lying too close for there to be any doubt on that score."

"That doesn't mean anything. My ex-husbands had healthy libidos, too. It didn't change how they felt about me. It didn't make them care—" Her voice broke.

Nick didn't think, he simply enfolded her in his arms. She resisted, as he'd known she would.

"Don't," she said. "I don't want your pity."

"Does this feel like pity?" He took her hand and pressed it to his erection, which was straining the fabric of his boxer shorts. "And don't tell me it doesn't mean anything. What do you think, that men are like dogs or pigs, that they'll respond on cue every time, no matter how great an aversion they have to the woman they're with?"

"I didn't say that, I just—" She tried to pull her hand away. He didn't let her. She gave a huff of annoyance. "You said it yourself. Men are always looking for another warm body, another conquest."

"And what sets us apart from the dogs and the pigs

is that sometimes we just look. I can't speak for those two clowns you married, but this—" he drew her hand up the length of his engorged penis, and down it "—is not some autonomic glandular response to the mere presence of a female. If you haven't figured out yet how outrageously attracted I am to you, then you're completely delusional."

Amanda went still. "Don't say that. It..."

"Complicates things. I know." Nick kissed her hard, pulling her under him, pressing her into the mattress. It was a demanding, possessive kiss, and he didn't let her up for air until she'd softened and begun to respond. And then he released her mouth only to feverishly yank at the buttons of her pajama top.

Amanda didn't try to stop him, and it was a good thing, because Nick wasn't sure he could stop. His hunger for her had slipped its leash, driving him, propelling him toward the inevitable. Roughly he pulled the silk top down her arms and off of her, hearing something rip. Her breath came in fast, agitated rasps. He knew he should slow down and do it right, but he was beyond that.

Nick pulled Amanda's pajama bottoms off just as swiftly, and his own boxer shorts, goaded by the perfume of her arousal, by the urgency of her soft hands on his body, by his own ungovernable need, too long denied.

She wrapped herself around him as he mounted her, as he pushed into her, into the astonishingly tight, slick depths of her. She gasped, and clung to him, and he groaned deep in his chest, overcome by the sharp, biting pleasure that rocketed through him.

She moaned his name, again and again, arching against him, bringing them even closer together. The bedcovers were tangled around them; automatically he kicked them away.

Sex had never been like this for Nick. Never before had reason fled so completely, to be replaced by pure mating instinct, the visceral, primordial need to join himself with another. He suspected the same was true for Amanda. She moved like a wild thing beneath him, locked into an age-old rhythm, uttering guttural, uninhibited sounds that pushed him right to the edge.

Amanda curled a leg around his thigh as if to lever herself over him. Nick easily rolled the two of them to position her on top. He still couldn't see her, but the impenetrable darkness only heightened the glut of sensation. Her slim thighs flexed under his fingers as she raised and lowered herself, drawing him into her slippery, welcoming heat. He slid his hands over her hips, her slender waist, up her rib cage and higher.

Her breath caught as he stroked those beautiful, dainty breasts and plucked the stiff tips. Her feminine muscles tightened around him, and he groaned and laughed at the same time, perilously close to climax.

He felt Amanda's fingers on his face, her touch soft and delicate as she traced his features. She stroked his eyelids and brushed her fingertips over his lashes. Her fingers moved down his nose and across his cheek, where they discovered his dimple.

"You're smiling," she said.

"I'm happy." His hands caressed her everywhere as the two of them moved in tandem. "I don't think I've ever been happier."

Her fingers lit on his mouth, as if to silence him. Perhaps she wanted to think of this as pure physical gratification, nothing more. A simple act of sex devoid of the threat posed by intimacy and emotional entanglements. His lips grasped her fingertip and his tongue teased it. A little sound escaped her. Her movements became faster, more frenzied. Clasping her hips, he angled them, and his own, so he'd stroke her in just the right place.

Amanda's hair whipped Nick's face. Urgent sounds escaped her as she reached for her release. He felt it gather in her, felt her body tense, and shudder, and rock under the force of it, felt her intimate flesh contract around him, urging him to let himself go.

Nick bucked hard under her, clamping his fingers around her hips, emptying himself in waves of pure scalding pleasure. She collapsed on top of him. After a moment they shifted to lie entwined, their lungs pumping like bellows, their hearts galloping in unison.

When Nick could speak, he said, "I think we can officially lay the Ice Queen label to rest."

Amanda laughed, much to Nick's relief. He'd half expected her to withdraw from him, weighed down by regret and fear of commitment. Perhaps she would, later, but for now, she was his.

And unbeknownst to her, he was that much closer to his goal.

She snuggled closer to him. He asked, "Are you cold?" They were both naked and damp with sweat, and the room was chilly.

She nodded and groped with her feet for the comforter he'd discarded earlier.

"I have a better idea," Nick said, and pulled her up with him.

A scant minute later, Amanda found herself standing under the hot spray of the shower with Nick. In the diffuse light filtering through the steam and the smoked-glass shower doors, he looked like sin incarnate, with his strong, finely hewn features, his swarthy coloring and that incandescent smile. Not to mention his powerful, perfectly proportioned body, revealed to her at last in its entirety.

Nick had the kind of muscle definition that resulted from hard work and a high-octane lifestyle, rather than hours a day spent lifting heavy things in a health club. His chest was wide and hard, with just the right amount of crisp dark hair, tapering over a flat, corrugated belly and thighs thick with sinew.

Amanda pushed her wet hair off her face and watched him roll the bar of soap in his hands, looking her over as if deciding where to start. She could have told him that certain parts of her were even now clamoring for his attention, but something told her that Nick would work his way around to them eventually.

He brought the clear, blue-green soap to his nose. It was a natural glycerine soap scented with a distinctive fragrance called Mist. She had it shipped to her regularly from a little shop in London. Nick's eyes held an appreciative glint as he said, "Smells like you. Turn around."

She did, letting the spray pummel her front as Nick spread lather on her back. His big hands moved in circles down to her waist and over the flare of her hips.

He murmured, "You're exquisite, Amanda."

The buzz of sensual awareness had never left her, and now it grew stronger as he lazily washed her, paying close attention to the sensitive skin of her bottom. His slippery fingers caressed her, kneaded the muscles, lightly skimmed up the rear cleft, sending an electric jolt through her.

Amanda leaned her palms on the tile wall and raised her face to the spray as Nick gave the same loving attention to her legs. Each time his fingers stroked up the insides of her thighs, they inched a little higher. She was trembling slightly when he turned her to face him.

Her gaze moved from the soap he was rolling between his palms, to his face. The hint of a smile touched his dark eyes, along with something else, something that caused a tingle of anticipation to race along every nerve ending.

Amanda felt almost drugged as she watched his hands, so dark and rough in contrast to her pale skin, slide up and down her arms, lathering them thoroughly, massaging each finger in turn. Slowly he rubbed the bar of soap across her shoulder and circled one breast, his intense gaze following its progress. She felt the nipple tighten, felt a voluptuous heaviness settle between her legs.

Never, during either of her marriages, had she
wanted to have sex twice in one night. Not that it had
ever been an issue, as both Roger and Ben had regularly lapsed into unconsciousness within seconds of
orgasm—almost always leaving her unsatisfied, a cir-
cumstance they had, naturally, blamed on her.

Now, for the first time ever, she was eager for a re-
peat performance. Amanda knew it had nothing to do
with her protracted period of abstinence. What she
and Nick had just shared was a first for her. If she'd
known it could be like that, she might never have tied
the knot with those two selfish bastards in the first
place.

Dropping her gaze, she saw that she wasn't the only
one ready for round number two. Nick remained ram-
pantly, unashamedly aroused as he smoothed lather
over both breasts with the painstaking care of a pastry
chef icing twin cakes. He paid special attention to the
erect peaks before directing his attention to her stomach, hips and thighs, leaving a frothy layer of bubbles
in his wake.

"When do I get my turn?" Amanda asked.

"I'm not finished." Nick proved it by pressing a
soapy hand between her legs, which immediately
threatened to buckle. "But if you'd rather I stopped..."

"No!" Amanda grabbed his shoulders for support
as his slick fingers began a leisurely exploration.
"Don't stop."

And he didn't. He caressed her with loving skill as
his other hand tipped her head back. He sipped at the
water trailing over her eyelids. He licked the droplets

clinging to her lips. She shivered. Her legs parted, of their own accord. So did her mouth. His tongue slipped between her lips as his fingers circled her most sensitive spot, wringing a groan of pure animal need from her.

Shamelessly Amanda rode his hand, rocking into his caress, clawing his shoulders, feeling the exquisite tension in her belly coil tighter and tighter.

In the next instant, Nick was lifting her and turning her, and bracing her back against the tile wall opposite the shower head as she instinctively wrapped her legs around his hips. He pressed into her in one long, smooth stroke, never taking his gaze from hers. Something passed between them then, something both frightening and exhilarating. In that instant Amanda knew that she'd been changed forever. No matter what the future held for her, Nick Stephanos had left his stamp.

Amanda had never experienced anything like the fierce, stabbing pleasure of taking Nick inside her body. It was a sensation so intense, it was akin to being turned inside out, body and soul.

The shower spray bounced off his back and her lower legs as he drove himself even deeper into her, holding her up with seeming effortlessness. The soapy lather between their bodies acted as an erotic lubricant between her sensitized breasts and the rough hair of his chest. Their mouths mated as enthusiastically as their bodies, his tongue thrusting and retreating in the same primal rhythm. Never in her life had Amanda felt so thoroughly, so ruthlessly, so deliciously possessed.

Nick relinquished her mouth at last, though the pace of his loving never slowed. "You're going to come more than once this time."

"I know."

His dimple was the last thing she saw before he lowered his mouth once more.

12

"WOULD YOU PASS that syrup down here?" Cousin Barb called, from way down the long row of diner tables that had been pushed together to accommodate the party of fourteen.

"Regular or blueberry?" Amanda asked.

"Strawberry."

"You got it."

Amanda had enjoyed Sunday breakfast at Wafflemania hundreds of times during the past thirty years, but never with a crowd this size. She and Nick had arrived at the diner a half hour earlier with her parents, grandparents, and Barb and her husband, Hal, only to find Sunny and Kirk, Raven and Hunter, and Charli and Grant already there, waiting for them.

Winter sunshine poured through the large windows of the diner's busy main room, highlighting every speck of dust on the plastic ferns hanging from the ceiling. Amanda always found this pedestrian setting, as well as the familiar aromas of greasy food and strong coffee, strangely comforting.

Nick sat next to her at the end of the long table. Eyeing her breakfast, he said, "I still can't believe you can be satisfied with a bowl of yogurt topped with granola and banana slices. And then there's..." He tapped her ever-present mug of jasmine tea.

"It's what I always order," she said. "This or a half cantaloupe with cottage cheese. Which doesn't happen to be in season at the moment."

He grinned. "I never knew you were such a creature of habit."

"What can I tell you? If I regularly ate what everyone else here is having—" she nodded toward Sunny's Belgian waffle crowned with vanilla ice cream and hot fudge, and Perry's three-egg western omelet with sausage, toast and home fries "—I'd weigh two hundred pounds."

Nick glanced at his own partially eaten breakfast: two fried eggs, a stack of pancakes and a pile of extra-crispy bacon. And plenty of black coffee. "I'll work this off walking around Manhattan taking pictures this afternoon." He met her gaze directly. "Why don't you join me."

A real date, in other words. Just the two of them, without the "audience" that had given a purpose to all their other get-togethers these past three months.

When she didn't respond, he added, "Come on—it'll be fun. Afterward we can check out this terrific Greek restaurant I found."

Amanda took a deep breath. Keeping her voice low, she said, "I don't think that would be a good idea, Nick."

His expression didn't change. It was as if he'd expected her refusal.

She wanted nothing more than to stroll around the

city with Nick today, chatting and laughing, watching him snap pictures, maybe buying a couple of New York City's famous "dirty water" hot dogs from a street vendor.

But that was one pleasure she couldn't allow herself. Not when she was so hopelessly conflicted. How had her cunning scheme managed to backfire so completely? Nick was a hired hand, for heaven's sake! She was paying him to do a job!

Last night had changed things irrevocably. Never one to delude herself, Amanda was forced to admit the astonishing, dismaying truth.

She'd fallen in love with the hired hand.

"Are you all right?" he asked.

"What? Yes. Of course." That was how their first conversation had started, she recalled, in his cab back in October, with Nick asking her if she was all right.

She frowned. Strange thing for a cabbie to ask, simply because she'd been muttering to herself. It was almost as if he'd been looking for some way to break the ice. But why? Certainly not to hit on her. He'd shown no sexual interest in her at all that day.

Amanda looked at Nick, now forking up a mouthful of pancake and listening to Liv, on his other side, describe the latest art exhibit at the Nassau County Museum, where she was an important donor. Amanda knew so much more about Nick now than when she'd initiated her fake-fiancé farce, but suddenly she had the uncomfortable feeling she didn't know him at all. Not in the ways that mattered most.

She watched as Mike, Sunny's surly former boss

here at Wafflemania, approached his onetime employee and started griping about the waitress who'd replaced her.

"I don't want to hear it," Sunny said. "You're just used to the way I did things, that's all. Give her a chance."

"She don't know how to work the tables when we're busy like this," he complained.

"So train her!" Sunny gave Mike a playful smack on the arm. "She hasn't had twelve years to get it right like I did."

Mike spread his hands. "Come back to work, Sunny. I'll raise you fifty cents an hour."

This was met with gales of laughter from everyone who knew the new Mrs. Kirk Larsen. As if she'd give up raising her stepson, Ian, and taking courses at the local university, just so she could go back to serving up the He-Man Special in that hideous Pepto-Bismol-colored, polyester waitress uniform.

Sunny gave him a consoling pat on the arm. "Work with her a little, Mike. She'll get the hang of it."

He shambled off, grumbling about the ingratitude of some people.

Amanda didn't like the knowing looks her parents and the others had been giving her and Nick all morning, as if they knew what the two of them had done last night. Had they heard something? Certainly she'd never been that uninhibited in her life. Just how thin were her walls?

Damn it! she thought, feeling her face heat. She had to get this blushing thing under control!

An hour and a half later, she and Nick stood in her driveway, waving to the last of her houseguests, her parents, as they pulled onto the road, headed back to New Jersey. Perry and Liv had been like young lovers last night and this morning, cuddling at every opportunity, sharing whispered endearments, stealing little kisses.

Amanda thought again about the role Nick had played in her parents' reconciliation. She was still so incredibly touched by his willingness to get involved, by his sincere concern for her and her family. Several days after that scene with Connor, Nick had delivered to Liv the balance of the money Connor had swindled her out of. Connor hadn't bothered her in the five weeks that had elapsed since then, and Nick seemed certain Liv had seen the last of him.

Once Nick and Amanda were back inside the house, he faced her. "You sure you won't join me in the city today? It's supposed to stay nice and mild like this all day."

"Nick." Amanda's gaze slid to the glass-topped console table and the pile of engagement presents her friends had forced her to unwrap. "Things have gotten a little...sidetracked."

He laughed!

She scowled at him. "This isn't funny."

"No, it's not funny, but how can you expect me to take you seriously when you come out with a statement like that after what we shared last night?"

She let out a long exhalation. "That was... It's so..."

His expression turned serious. "Are you telling me you regret it?"

Amanda couldn't lie. "No. How could I regret..." She closed her eyes for a long moment, gathering her thoughts. "You gave me something last night, Nick. I don't know how to explain it. You showed me something about myself and..." She offered a bittersweet smile. "Well, let's just say I'll never again blame myself for other people's, shall we say, inadequacies."

A smile tugged at his mouth. "In the bedroom."

"Or in the shower." She couldn't restrain a full-fledged grin.

"Amanda, you have more passion and feeling and—" he groped for the right word "—and *heart* than anyone I know. How could you have ever sold yourself short?"

His assessment warmed her, but it didn't change the basic facts. "I don't regret what we did, but we—we can't let it happen again. In a few days..." Amanda took a second to compose herself. "In, uh, let's say a week, ten days, I'll tell my friends that we've called off the wedding."

He said nothing, but his dark eyes never left her face. She directed her gaze to the cluster of landscape watercolors over her modular sofa. "Nothing has changed between us," she said.

Nick's voice was quiet and certain. "You can tell yourself that all you want, but it doesn't change the facts." She tried to turn away; he held her shoulders and made her face him. "Things *have* changed between us, Amanda. I love you."

"No, don't—"

His fingers tightened on her. "I love you and I'm pretty sure you love me. It wasn't part of your grand scheme, but it happened and we're going to confront it." He released her. "You're not the type to deny the obvious. Don't start now."

Amanda dropped into the nearest chair, a sleek, contemporary armchair upholstered in pale peach raw silk. She cradled her head in her hands.

Slowly he knelt in front of her. He pulled her hands away and held them in his. "What are you afraid of, Amanda?"

She pulled in a shaky breath. She looked at him. "I know now that losing Roger, and Ben, well, they were no great loss. But with you..."

He squeezed her hands, mutely urging her to finish her thought.

"It *is* scary," she admitted. Tears pricked at her eyes. "I keep wondering how long...how long it will take you to discover how unlovable I really am."

"Oh, honey—"

"Nick, I know how pathetic that sounds. I'm not trying to go for high drama here, I just want you to understand." In a small voice she said, "I don't have a very good track record when it comes to choosing men. You already know all about that."

"Well, you've obviously improved." His smile was teasing. "You chose me."

She smirked, even as she wiped her eyes with her fingertips. "That doesn't count. You're playing a role."

"I *was* playing a role. Somewhere along the line, it became real life. For you, too. You have feelings for me. Don't deny it."

"I won't. I can't. Last night never would've happened if I didn't care for you."

"Well, see, now we *have* to get married."

"I know we didn't use any birth control, but it's a little soon to make a pronouncement like that, don't you think?"

"I'm not talking about pregnancy, I'm talking about that unfortunate habit of yours."

Her brow wrinkled. "That unfortunate... Oh, you mean..."

"You sleep with a guy, you drag him to the altar. And we've already established you're a creature of habit." He spread his arms in a well-here-I-am gesture.

Amanda couldn't help laughing. How did the man manage it? She could be practically slitting her wrists and he'd find a way to jolly her out of it.

"We have the date," Nick continued, "the J.P., the guest list, the band. The flowers are ordered, so are the invitations, and the menu's set. We don't even have to go shopping for a ring." He indicated his grandmother's platinum-and-diamond filigree ring, which Amanda had worn almost constantly since he'd placed it on her finger two weeks earlier. "The only thing we have to decide on is the honeymoon. I vote for Lake Tahoe. If you can't ski, I'll teach you."

She stared at him. "You're serious."

"As far as I'm concerned, this wedding's a go."

"You're certifiable! This is a *fake* engagement, Nick, remember? It's not for real!"

Quietly he said, "Why couldn't it be?"

Amanda swallowed hard. "This is so... We can't just..."

"Everything's all settled. Including the most important part." He took her hands again. "Which is that I love you and I want to spend the rest of my life with you. And you love me." His expression dared her to deny it.

"Yes." Her voice was wobbly. "I love you."

The gentlest smile touched his eyes. "Then marry me."

It sounded so sensible when he put it like that, so right. She averted her face. It was difficult enough to try to make sense of all this, but when she was staring into those warm, dark chocolate eyes of his...

"Amanda."

She looked at him.

"I'm not those other losers," he said. "All I can tell you is it's a good thing Roger and Ben made themselves scarce, because if they hadn't, I'd have had to kill them to get to you."

Giddy laughter bubbled forth from Amanda. How had she lived the first thirty years of her life without this remarkable man in her life?

Could she really go through with this?

Her thoughts must have been plain on her face. "Third time's the charm," Nick said. "At least, that's what I've heard."

She couldn't do worse than the last two times. But

mostly, she couldn't bear the thought of letting Nick walk out of her life in a week or two.

She said, "I must be crazy."

"Sanity is highly overrated. What'll it be, Amanda? Don't make me stand here all alone on March tenth with my boutonniere getting limp."

She responded with a bark of laughter.

"Ah, the lady's snorting. That's always a good sign."

"Yes," she said, grinning so hard her face hurt. "We're both probably certifiable, but yes, Nick, yes, I'll marry you."

13

"WHEN WILL YOU GET the pictures back?" Amanda shed her down-filled suede jacket and glanced around Nick's apartment. He took it from her and hung it on a coat tree in the corner, along with his navy peacoat.

"I'll take the film to the lab tomorrow morning," he said. "I should have them Tuesday."

"I'm dying to see how the ones I took of that fence come out."

There was an iron fence in lower Manhattan that had been there since colonial times. During the Revolutionary War, American soldiers had knocked off the finials, which had been shaped as symbols of the British monarchy. The fence had been repainted regularly since then, but one could still see the irregular tops of some of the fenceposts where the finials had been removed.

Using Nick's camera, Amanda had taken pictures of the fence from various angles, as well as other details of New York City's historical architecture, while Nick had concentrated on photographing people. Between them, she felt they'd captured the essence of the city.

After agreeing to marry Nick—for real this time—she'd gladly accompanied him on his jaunt into the city. It had been a long, exhausting, thoroughly enjoyable day. They'd covered a good part of lower Manhattan on foot and gone through four rolls of film. And yes, they'd lunched al fresco on dirty-water hot dogs, later dining at the wonderful Greek restaurant Nick had told her about.

Amanda could be herself with Nick. She didn't have to be Amanda Coppersmith, CEO. She didn't have to be Amanda Coppersmith, arbiter of style and taste. Most of all, she didn't have to be Amanda Coppersmith, Ice Queen.

Nick appreciated her, the real her, as no man ever had. They'd explored the city and held hands and fed each other hot dogs and made faces for the camera and planned their honeymoon, and she couldn't remember ever having enjoyed a day more.

Coming up behind Amanda now, Nick slipped his arms around her waist and nuzzled her neck. She smiled, leaned back into him and turned her face up for his kiss. His lips felt soft and cool.

"How about some hot chocolate?" he asked.

"You're going to make me fat. All this eating."

His hands roved over her stomach and hips, sending a thrill of expectation through her, sparking memories of last night. "An extra pound or two wouldn't hurt."

She smiled. "Ah, the criticism starts already."

"Never. You're perfect, Amanda. You'll always be perfect, even if you gain a hundred pounds."

"Good answer."

His arms tightened around her, fractionally. In a sober tone he said, "We need to talk about something."

She turned a little to see him better. He wore the strangest sad smile. "This sounds serious. Should I be worried?"

He didn't answer immediately, and Amanda felt her pulse quicken. "Nick?"

He gave her another light kiss and released her. "It's not like that—nothing to worry about. I'll get the milk heated up. I make my hot chocolate from scratch—you'll like it. It'll be a couple of minutes, then we'll talk."

Amanda watched him disappear into the kitchen. Whatever was on his mind, she wasn't worried. Nick was the most candid, most sincere guy she knew. Whatever he wanted to discuss, it couldn't be too earth-shattering.

She strolled around his living room, examining the South American tapestry and the black-and-white photographs displayed over the low, burled-wood cabinet. He'd added a couple of pictures since she was last here over two months earlier. She ran her fingers along the glossy top of the cabinet, once again impressed by the craftsmanship. From the kitchen came the sounds of the refrigerator opening and closing, a pot banging against the stove.

A large, leather-bound book sat on the end of the cabinet, some sort of album. More of his photos, no doubt. Flipping it open to the first page, Amanda was surprised to see that the two five-by-sevens displayed there were in color, not black and white. And they weren't slices of city life but front and back views of eight identical wooden chairs, lined up in a row. The chairs had clean Shaker-type lines but a bit more style, and were made of some pale wood. They lacked seat cushions but otherwise were ready for someone's dining room.

Why did Nick have pictures of chairs in his photo album? She turned to the next page and saw an armoire made of dark walnut, photographed from various angles. The next set of pictures showed a coffee table and matching lamp table.

Nick called from the kitchen, "How sweet do you like your hot chocolate?"

"Not overly," she replied. "More chocolatey than sugary."

"Good, that's how I like it, too."

She started to ask about the album, but her voice was drowned out by the whine of a blender.

Turning to the next page in the album, Amanda saw photographs of the very cabinet she stood before.

"Oh!" This had to be a portfolio displaying furniture Nick had constructed, probably to give prospective customers an idea of his skill. He'd told her he did a little carpentry on the side, a laughably modest description of his work, she now realized. These pieces had been executed by a true artisan.

The next few pages contained photos of a built-in bookcase—probably the one in his bedroom that he'd squabbled with Mrs. Konstantopoulos over—a desk, and a diminutive child's table-and-chair set. She turned the page and froze.

The shock of recognition stole Amanda's breath. She knew that cedar chest. There couldn't be two like it. It was massive, with rounded edges, decorative joints and distinctive, heavy brass hardware.

And it belonged to her brother, Jared.

More precisely, it belonged to Jared's wife, Noelle. Jared had commissioned the piece for his bride-to-be five and a half years ago, just before his wedding. Amanda had been present when the piece was delivered to her brother's home. She'd never seen anything like that hand-crafted chest, which was exquisitely detailed and redolent with the heavenly scent of fresh-cut cedar. Even now, as she held the photos in her hands, she could almost smell the sweet, woodsy aroma.

Nick had made this chest for Jared. Which meant that—

"Do you want nutmeg?" Nick called.

—the two men had already met each other, years before she'd introduced them at her birthday party.

Her heart slammed into her rib cage.

Nick yelled from the kitchen, "Amanda?"

The chest had been delivered by the craftsman himself, she recalled. The man had dark hair, longer than Nick currently wore it. He'd carried the heavy chest without assistance; ropy muscles had stood out in his arms. She didn't remember much more about him, because her attention had been on his splendid workmanship. She'd opened the chest, breathed deeply of its perfume, run her hands over the smooth surface of the wood, tracing the reddish striations of the grain.

At the time, she'd thought of Nick not as a mere carpenter but as an artisan, a woodworking genius who employed old-world techniques to create magnificent, one-of-a-kind pieces like that cedar chest.

Amanda didn't look up from the photos as Nick came into the room. He said, "You didn't say, so I gave you a sprinkle of nutmeg." She heard him set the mugs on the coffee table. "What have you got there?" he asked.

Then there was only silence. She looked up and saw him standing close. He lifted his somber gaze from the album to her face.

"It wasn't a chance meeting." Amanda felt the blood drain from her face. She stared at him, her eyes wide and unblinking. "That day back in October. It was no accident that I found myself in your cab."

"No," he said quietly. "It was no accident. Amanda, let me—"

"It was a setup from the beginning. I was supposed to think you were just—" Her throat constricted. She felt woozy. "And I fell for it. I walked right into it."

"Amanda, please..." He reached for her arm.

She shook him off and staggered to the coat tree. Suddenly she couldn't seem to fill her lungs; she had to get out of there.

"It wasn't my idea to do it that way," he said, as she grabbed her jacket and purse. "But they didn't give me any choice."

They? Jared was involved in this somehow. She remembered asking Raven, Sunny and Charli if they'd enlisted her brother in whatever scheme they were cooking up. They must have found Nick through him. "The Wedding Ring did this," she said dully. "They were behind it from the beginning."

Nick nodded, his dark gaze troubled. "I was waiting for you in my taxi that day, parked near your office building with my off-duty light on. As soon as I saw you come out, I went on duty and pulled up."

She recalled how ridiculously easy it had been to hail a cab that day. And how preoccupied she'd been with working out the details of the plan she'd just hatched—the most important detail of which was finding a suitable man to pose as her boyfriend.

Her Wedding Ring pals had outmaneuvered her! They knew her so well, they were able to anticipate the scheme she would come up with. *That* had been their strategy all along, to use her own phony-boyfriend ploy to their advantage!

And it had worked like a charm. They'd cornered her in her office that day, tried to bully her into cooperating with their matchmaking plans, and she'd responded just the way they'd known she would, with a devious scheme to get around the rules of the pact they'd made twelve years earlier.

They'd deceived her. Raven. Sunny. Charli.

Nick.

She pulled the jacket on with jerky motions as she headed for the door.

"Amanda, don't leave. Listen to me."

She turned toward him, her hand on the doorknob. "I trusted you, Nick. I—I laid myself open for you, shared things I've never told anyone." Her chest felt painfully tight. "I loved you. How could you keep this from me?"

"I didn't want to. I wish it hadn't been necessary."

"Want to know the funny part?" Tears burned her eyelids. "I felt guilty for deceiving all of *them!*"

"Amanda—"

"They were constantly throwing us together, with all those double dates, and I'd laugh to myself, thinking it seemed like some kind of conspiracy! I guess the joke's on me, huh?" She opened the door. "You're wrong, Nick. I'm no better a judge of character than I was before. But at least my ex-husbands never plotted against me."

Nick watched the door slam closed behind Amanda. He listened to her hurried footfalls on the stairs. Crossing to the window, he watched her exit the building under the glare of a streetlamp and stride swiftly down the sidewalk and out of view.

It was about nine at night. They'd taken his car into the city and then here to Astoria. He'd been planning to drive her home in the morning. He assumed she now intended to hail a cab. It wouldn't be easy. This wasn't Manhattan; there just weren't that many taxis cruising for fares out here.

He pulled himself away from the window. His gaze landed on the coffee table and the mugs of hot chocolate sitting there, rapidly cooling.

She needed time. Fighting back the overwhelming impulse to run after her, to make her listen to reason, he carried the mugs to the kitchen and emptied them into the sink.

He braced his arms on the countertop. Closed his eyes. Struggled to shut off the inner voice that screamed at him to go after her. She wasn't receptive to what he had to say right now. She was too upset. She needed time to calm down, to think about all this.

Time to convince herself that he was no better than those worthless SOBs she'd married, time to shore up the walls of the emotional prison she'd just begun to crawl out of.

"The hell with it," he growled, and took off running.

Nick caught up to her two blocks away, in front of a small grocery store. She was walking stiffly, with her hands jammed in her pockets. He grabbed her arm, only to have her spin angrily around and pull away from him.

"Leave me alone!" she cried, her breath smoking in the cold.

"Don't you want to know why they chose *me?*" He stabbed his chest with a finger. "Aren't you even curious?"

Amanda tried to pass him; he blocked her path. She scowled as she took in his sweater. "You aren't even wearing a jacket. You're crazy. It's below freezing out here."

He said, "I fell in love with you the day I first set eyes on you."

"Right." Her tone was scathing. "The day you picked me up in your cab and manipulated me into choosing you for the role of phony boyfriend."

"No. Five and a half years ago. The day I brought that cedar chest to Jared's house."

Amanda went still.

"Your brother introduced us that day." Nick hugged himself against the cold. "I watched you examine that chest that I'd put so much effort into. I saw the way you looked at it, the way you touched it, with this kind of reverent appreciation. You asked me a lot of questions about it, what type of joints I used, how I finished it, that sort of thing."

"But I didn't recognize you, that day you picked me up in the cab."

"I didn't expect you to. It was a long time ago, and we only spoke for a few minutes. There was no reason for you to make the connection five and a half years later. But I never forgot you." He stamped his feet and tried to rub warmth into his hands. "You were so sweet and open when I met you that day at Jared's. Also sophisticated and smart as a whip, of course, but unpretentious, too. I liked that. And you were wearing a wedding ring." He blew warm air on his hands. "That, I didn't like."

Though it was late, the store they were standing in front of was still doing a brisk business. Nick steered Amanda away from the busy doorway.

"I was still married to Roger back then," she said. "That was, what, June or July?"

"Early August."

"Our marriage was on the skids by then, but I was trying to hang on, trying to..."

Trying to be a better wife. Trying to make him love me. She didn't say it. She didn't have to.

"I didn't know any of that," Nick said. "All I knew was that you were a married woman. Tough luck for me. After you left, I told Jared that if you happened to find yourself single, I was interested."

"I found myself single a little over a year later."

"And promptly ran into the arms of husband number two."

She grimaced. "It was too soon. I should've given myself more time."

"Then when you and Ben called it quits, your brother chose not to alert me, even though he thinks I'm a swell guy and would make a great brother-in-law. He knew you needed to get your head together. He knew you'd gone through hell and he didn't want to see you make the same mistake you did with Ben— hooking up with the wrong guy on the rebound."

"He didn't have to worry. I'd sworn off marriage for good. The last thing I wanted was a serious relationship."

"Which is where the Wedding Ring comes in."

"Which the prospective groom isn't supposed to know about. Or my brother, for that matter."

Nick's face was stiff with cold, but he managed a lopsided smile. "Let's just say this particular case presented its own set of challenges. Your friends decided to bend the rules."

"What did they do, ask Jared for help in finding a husband for me?"

Nick nodded. "Can we go back to my place? I can't feel my feet."

"Didn't it seem strange to you, being asked by virtual strangers to participate in such a bizarre, convoluted scheme?"

He shrugged. "Jared said those three women knew you better than anyone. And according to them, this bizarre, convoluted scheme was the only way I was going to get close to you in this lifetime, seeing as how you'd decided all boys have the cooties." He was trembling so hard from the cold, his teeth chattered. "Can we go back to the apartment now? *Please?*"

Distractedly Amanda began to retrace her steps. Nick put his arm around her back and hurried her along.

"How do you know Jared?" she asked.

"We met at a party about eight years ago. We go fishing once in a while, play a little poker. When he wanted a cedar chest built, he knew the guy to call."

"I saw you two having a little tête-à-tête at Hunter and Raven's Halloween party. The two of you made quite a striking pair, you in your Samson getup and Jared done up as Pinocchio with a glandular disorder. I wondered what you guys were chatting about."

"We were discussing my progress toward attaining my goal."

"Your goal?"

"You." He glanced at her as they crossed an intersection. "Your brother was afraid I'd blow my cover and get us both in hot water with your Wedding Ring pals. I assured him you didn't suspect a thing."

"I didn't," she grumbled.

"Believe me, I wasn't thrilled about having to engage in subterfuge to get you, but I figured if that was what it took, then that was what I'd do."

Her expression remained implacable.

"Amanda, think about it. Your friends didn't do anything you didn't try yourself. Both you and they resorted to devious manipulation. Only they did it better. Is that what burns you about this?"

No response.

"Or is it the fact that they took control away from you, by forcing you to honor the matchmaking pact you entered into in good faith?"

She sighed disgustedly. "There it is again, the old control-freak issue."

Nick produced his keys from his pocket. "The bottom line is they did this for you, Amanda. If you could get past the 'control-freak issue,' you'd see that."

He sensed her gaze on him as he unlocked the outer door between Benny's Clubhouse Tavern and the party supply store next to it. He turned to see the hint of a smile.

She said, "I almost burst a blood vessel when Charli's brother Paul recognized you. I thought the jig was up for sure."

"I managed to explain it away."

"Right. A cabbie who looks and sounds just like you! That separated-at-birth nonsense."

Nick ushered her into the building and up the stairs. "Honey, I could've announced that a taxi-driving alien had inhabited my body and your pals would've gone right along with it, because—"

"I know. Because everyone was in on it but me. I wondered why no one challenged you. And how you'd become such a slick liar."

"Didn't I tell you I'm a man of many talents?" He held the apartment door open for her.

"This is what you wanted to talk to me about tonight, isn't it?"

"Yes." He sighed. "This morning, when you agreed to marry me, it just wasn't the right time. And today, running around the city... I wanted to wait until we had some quiet time together."

"I think it would've been a shock no matter when I found out." Amanda unzipped her jacket.

Nick was still shivering with cold. Slowly she approached him, wrapped her arms around him. Gratefully he hauled her close, drowning in her warmth, her sweetness, her forgiveness.

She looked up at him. "Remember on New Year's Eve when you said you were a typical unromantic male?"

"Mm-hmm..." He nuzzled her cold, fragrant hair.

"You were wrong. I can't think of anything more romantic than waiting five and a half years for a woman, and then willingly entering into an insane conspiracy like this just for the chance to get close to her." Her eyes glistened. "If I live to be a hundred, I'll never find a man more devoted, more steadfast." Her voice cracked as she said, "I love you so much, Nick."

He smiled down at her. "Does this mean the wedding's back on?"

"The wedding's back on." She gave a watery chuckle. "But I'm warning you right now, our grandchildren are never going to believe this story."

14

AMANDA COULDN'T SAY HOW they ended up on the boldly patterned Asian rug, with the coffee table shoved out of the way. Her jacket came off as they writhed in a tangle, their mouths locked in a deep, hard, hungry kiss.

Nick's cable-knit sweater was cold to the touch. She thrust her hands under it, yanked up his undershirt, eager for the feel of his smooth, hot skin. She found herself beneath him, luxuriating in the raw eroticism of his weight pressing her into the firm, nubbly carpet. The most intimate parts of her thrummed with sensual anticipation.

He held himself over her, staring into her eyes, his own alight with wonder and love. His fingers threaded through her hair, making her scalp tingle. "You look very exotic like this, lying on an Oriental carpet with your blond hair spread out around you. Kind of like a harem slave."

She laughed. "Complete with turtleneck and jeans."

"Well, we can do something about that."

"That was what I was hoping you'd say."

Rising to his knees, straddling her hips, Nick unfastened her belt buckle and unzipped her black jeans. He pulled her pink cashmere turtleneck up and worked it over her head. "I was wrong," he said, with an appreciate smile. "Didn't I say your bra would be satin?" His hands molded the cups of her demi bra. His thumbs stroked her nipples, clearly visible through the sheer taupe lace. "Not that I'm complaining."

He swung off of Amanda and pulled off her half boots and socks as she wriggled out of her jeans. He smoothed his hand over her belly, tickling her navel with a fingertip. "I was right about the bikini panties, though." They were abbreviated string bikinis in matching taupe lace.

"You know what you should be wearing right now?" he asked, caressing her all over, causing a shiver of carnal awareness everywhere he touched. "That Delilah outfit. I fantasized about stripping that thing off of you during the whole Halloween party."

She raised one eyebrow. "You sure it wasn't Madame Hertz and her studded leather corset that had you all hot and bothered?"

"What can I tell you? I like a little something left to the imagination. And what I imagined doing to you after I got that thing off you..." His touch became bolder. Nick stroked a fingertip along the top of her low-cut bra. He undid the front fastening and spread it open, exposing her to his smoky gaze.

Nick pulled the bra off and tossed it aside. He hooked his fingers in her panties and slowly worked them down her hips and legs. Lying before him completely naked on that striking Asian rug, with him fully clothed, Amanda almost felt like the harem slave he'd compared her to, a pale and trembling concubine at the mercy of her swarthy captor.

She smiled, and his dimple showed in response. "What's so funny?" he demanded.

"I was just thinking that sex with you isn't likely to ever get boring."

Nick's gaze went from smoky to scorching as he leaned on an elbow and gave her body a leisurely perusal. "I think that's a safe assumption." One fingertip circled the tip of her breast. He watched in fascination as it puckered. "Your nipples are the most beautiful shade of pink. They're irresistible."

He proved it by lowering his head and lightly touching his lips to it. Amanda's breath hitched. He pressed another soft kiss there, and another. She was astounded at how sensitive she was with Nick. He seemed to know just how to touch her, in stark contrast to her ex-husbands, who'd engaged in just enough clumsy foreplay to ensure their own arousal.

Nick touched the tip of his tongue to the other stiff, aching peak. She uttered his name on a whimpering sigh, clutched handfuls of his short hair to hold him to her. He took his time, tormenting her with short little licks that seemed to pluck some invisible cord connected to the deepest, hungriest part of her. Restlessly she squirmed beneath him, yearning for him to suckle harder, to roll on top of her and take her. Yet he continued to delicately taste her, tease her, until she had to bite her lip to keep from begging him to end her misery.

Nick raised his head at last. He studied her expression, and she knew what he saw: her panting mouth, her flared nostrils, the burning flush of arousal on her face and chest. He kissed her, a fleeting brush of his lips on hers. She tried to rise, tried to hold on to his mouth. Gently he pushed her back down, his small smile telling her to trust him.

His fingers slid into the patch of tawny hair between her legs. It was all Amanda could do to lie still. Her body flexed, her legs fell open, as he found the moist petals. Reaching for him, she grasped his sweater sleeve and held on as he touched a fingertip to her saturated opening. Her breath fled in a ragged sigh. His finger pushed, and entered her, slowly, deeply. Her hips rocked to the thrusting cadence of his caress. A second finger followed, filling her more completely as his thumb lightly brushed her clitoris.

Amanda's mouth opened on a silent cry as reason and conscious thought deserted her, to be replaced by pure physical sensation. Just when her release began to build, Nick drew his hand away. He slid lower, settled between her legs. Amanda felt his hot breath there. Her entire being tightened with a thrill of expectation.

She gasped his name as his rough fingers parted her. Then his first searing kiss knocked the breath from her lungs and she could say nothing, do nothing except whip her head from side to side and wonder giddily if she could withstand the startling pleasure of it.

Nick loved her with his mouth, patiently, slowly, until she was thrashing beneath him in a frenzy of sensual overload, all but wrestling with him as he held her hips in a firm grip. His tongue darted and stabbed, alternating with long, lazy licks. His strong, supple mouth tugged at her most sensitive flesh, until she was practically sobbing with the unadulterated pleasure of it, with the blinding, all-consuming need to join her body with his, to take him deep within herself.

His tongue flicked rapidly, burning her, forcing her ever closer to the climax steadily building within her. He never ceased the rapid-fire lashing, even as his fingers burrowed and thrust, sending her over the edge. Her orgasm ripped hoarse screams from her throat; it bowed her body and became her world, blocking out all else.

Before the pulsating pleasure had wound down, Nick was there, on top of her, and she opened to him, to the glorious pressure as he stretched her, filled her, touched the deepest recesses of her. She rose to meet him, the two of them moving as one. He was still dressed, and that excited her. Everything about him excited her—his fierce expression, the vein that pulsed at his temple, the bunching of his muscles as she clawed at his hard waist.

Kneeling, Nick lifted her onto his lap and wrapped her legs around his hips. He stroked her at a different angle now, raising and lowering her with one hand as he lifted her breast. He drew the erect peak into his mouth, wringing a moan of pleasure from her. He nipped her, and suckled hard, and she felt it there, where they were joined.

"Nick," Amanda gasped. "Nick...now..." The moment of release was upon her, and she wanted to share it with him.

"I'm with you, honey." He kissed her mouth. "I'm right with you."

She watched him as the exquisite pressure built within her, within them both. She watched Nick's expressive face as the pressure mounted, and peaked, and spilled over, seizing them in its jaws, shaking them like rag dolls. All they could do was hold on to each other and ride it out.

They sat like that for a long time, clinging to each other, letting the aftershocks roll over them. Amanda kissed Nick's neck and felt him twitch within her. She smiled, and deposited a trail of kisses up his throat to his jaw, rough with beard stubble.

"Something tells me we're not through for the evening," she murmured.

"Not by a long shot, honey."

She kissed his smiling mouth. "Amazing, isn't it?"

"That once isn't enough? How decrepit do you think I am?"

"No, I mean that the scheme my Wedding Ring pals concocted was so spectacularly successful. *I'm* supposed to be the devious one! I don't know whether to thank them for giving me you, or to slap them silly for playing such a dirty trick on me."

"Oh, I have a feeling that by the morning, you'll forget all about the dirty trick and only want to shower those ladies with your most profound, heartfelt and everlasting gratitude."

"You mean once I've had a chance to sleep on it?"

Nick gave her that megawatt grin, along with a little hip thrust that told her that once was, indeed, not enough. "Who said anything about sleeping?"

_____Epilogue_____

Despite all the meticulous planning, Amanda's third and final trek down the aisle offered a bit more excitement than anyone had anticipated. The furnace in her basement chose that day to go on the fritz; the sound of clanging pipes competed with the Wedding March as the repairman worked to restore heat. Meanwhile, the fire blazing in the living room hearth did little to drive off the mid-March chill. Most of the guests kept their coats on during the ceremony.

A blizzard the day before had shut down local airports and prevented a dozen out-of-town relatives from attending. The justice of the peace arrived forty-five minutes late, although he'd had to travel less than two miles over plowed roads. Then, just as the wedding was about to start, a seam opened in Amanda's gown, a belted, ankle-length column of wheat-colored jersey whose skirt was covered in clear sequins. Thank goodness Charli was so handy with a needle and thread.

When things finally got under way, the flower girl, Jared and Noelle's four-year-old daughter, Janine, decided that the words "we are gathered" was the cue to throw a kicking, shrieking tantrum. This set off Raven and Hunter's two-week-old daughter, Annabel, who until then had been peacefully dozing on her father's shoulder.

"Remind me never to do this again," Amanda groaned hours later, as she plopped onto her sofa and kicked off her high-heeled silver sling-backs.

"You'll never get a chance to do this again." Settling next to her, Nick draped his arm around her shoulders. He lifted her left hand and kissed her ring finger. "Now that I've got you, I'm never letting you go."

The last of their guests had departed, except for the members of the Wedding Ring and their husbands, who'd joined the bride and groom in the den for one last glass of champagne as the rent-a-maids cleaned up the kitchen and living and dining rooms. The heat was back on, thankfully, and all Amanda wanted to do now was relax with her new husband and her best friends, and decompress.

Raven had just nursed her tiny daughter, who was now awake and alert, cradled in her mother's arms and avidly taking in her surroundings.

Kirk said, "That's a beautiful name. Annabel. How did you choose it?"

Hunter was sitting on the floor next to his wife's chair. He offered his daughter his finger and she grasped it firmly. "Raven and I are both fans of Edgar Allan Poe. She was named for his poem 'Annabel Lee.'"

The gurgle Annabel emitted sounded so much like enthusiastic approval that everyone laughed.

"Well, she's a beauty." Reverently Grant touched

Charli's abdomen, gently swelling with their growing child. "In five months or so, she'll have a playmate."

"You feeling okay?" Amanda asked Charli.

"Terrific. A little morning sickness in the beginning, but I'm fine now."

Hunter said, "How's the practice working out, Grant?"

"Better than I'd hoped. I won't kid you. It's scary as hell hanging out a shingle when all you've known is a regular paycheck, but it was a choice between starting my own firm or going back to the D.A.'s office, and when it came down to it, there was really no contest."

Grant's obsessive desire to become a partner in the ultraconservative law firm he'd worked for had led him to marry Charli for appearances' sake, a practical, platonic arrangement that had nothing in common with the warmly loving marriage they now shared. His recent failure to make partner might have devastated him if he hadn't had the emotional support and devotion of his wife. Rather than wallow in self-pity, Grant had responded by starting his own law firm, in partnership with a buddy of his. As tough and risky as that was, he felt it beat spending the next twenty or thirty years working his tail off for his old firm, only to retire as a senior associate.

Two-year-old Ian was napping on Sunny's lap. Idly stroking his blond hair, she said to Raven, "Your pregnancy gave you some great material for your stand-up comedy routines at Stitches. What are you going to do now that you don't have the built-in hilarity of a gigantic belly?"

"Never fear. Between the Chernobyl diapers, gnawed nipples and *Night of the Living Dead* sleep deprivation, caring for a newborn has more than its share of comic potential. It's one of those if-you-don't-laugh-you'll-cry situations, so I may as well laugh."

Hunter said, "We keep a notepad handy to jot down ideas for gags, once Raven's up to performing again."

"You can remind me of the laughing part about eight months from now," Sunny said. Every female in the room gasped, and she grinned like the cat that got the cream. "It happened during our belated honeymoon last month."

Kirk kissed his wife. "She just took the test. It's positive."

Sunny's friends were all over her, hugging her and crying happy tears. They knew how much becoming a mother meant to her. She adored her stepson, Ian, and had resigned herself to the fact that their family might not grow any larger. Then Kirk had had his vasectomy reversed in October, and apparently the surgery had been a success.

Raven said, "Three Wedding Ring babies!" She winked at Amanda. "It's your turn now."

Nick laughed. "You'll be the first to know."

Amanda and Nick had been careless about birth control, and when her period was a few days late last month, Amanda had found herself actually hoping that she was pregnant with Nick's baby. That false alarm had led them to a frank discussion about children—and the decision to forgo contraception and let nature take its course. Her house—Nick's house now, too—was certainly roomy enough for a gigantic brood, but they planned to limit their family to two kids. Well, perhaps three.

Amanda addressed her Wedding Ring pals. "I have a question. That guy you tried to set me up with, back in October. James Selden. The real estate developer. Does he really exist?"

Sunny shifted Ian in her arms. Smirking, she asked, "What do you think?"

Raven said, "I invented him on the spur of the moment to put pressure on you and provide incentive for you to hurry up and manufacture a fake boyfriend."

"Which you were confident I'd do," Amanda said, with an incredulous head shake. She still couldn't get over how thoroughly these three had predicted her actions. It was eerie.

"All you needed was a suitable fellow to dangle in front of us," Charli said. Smiling, she nodded toward Nick. "So we provided one ready-made."

Grant said, "Amanda, I didn't have a clue who you were talking about that day in the orchard when you mentioned my golfing buddy James. Then you said something about these three trying to set you up with the guy, so I did some quick thinking and figured I'd better play along or I'd be eating TV dinners for a month. Was I convincing?"

"You were all remarkably convincing," Amanda said. "I had no idea my best friends could be so cunning, so calculating, so incredibly underhanded. Gosh, you make me proud."

Charli said, "We learned a few things from you over the years."

"And it all ended happily," Sunny decreed.

"Amen to that," Raven said, giving her daughter a big, noisy kiss on the cheek.

"The time has come to officially disband the Wedding Ring," Sunny said, as Ian blinked and yawned in her arms.

Charli took her husband's hand. "That's so sad."

"Not really," Raven said. "The Wedding Ring has done its job. It's accomplished what we wanted it to."

Nick stood, champagne flute in hand. "I propose a toast. Gentlemen?" Hunter, Grant and Kirk came to their feet, glasses raised. "To four of the most accomplished practitioners in the history of matchmaking."

"Not to mention sexy," Kirk amended.

"And intriguing," Grant added.

Hunter nodded. "And funny."

Nick's dimple showed. "Let us not forget exasperating."

"You can stop now," Amanda said dryly.

The four men clinked their glasses in unison. *"To the Wedding Ring!"*

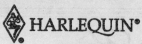

Finding Home

New York Times bestselling authors

Linda Howard
Elizabeth Lowell
Kasey Michaels

invite you on
the journey of a lifetime.

Three women are searching—
each wants a place to belong,
a man to care for her,
a child to love.

Will her wishes be fulfilled?

*Coming in April 2001
only from Silhouette Books!*

Silhouette®
Where love comes alive™

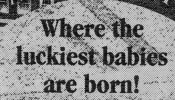

MAITLAND MATERNITY

Where the luckiest babies are born!

In April 2001, look for

HER BEST FRIEND'S BABY

by Vicki Lewis Thompson

A car accident leaves surrogate mother Mary-Jane Potter's baby-to-be without a mother—

and causes the father, Morgan Tate, to fuss over a very pregnant Mary-Jane like a mother hen. Suddenly, Mary-Jane is dreaming of keeping the baby…and the father!

Each book tells a different story about the world-renowned Maitland Maternity Clinic— where romances are born, secrets are revealed… and bundles of joy are delivered.

INDULGE IN A QUIET MOMENT
WITH HARLEQUIN

Get a FREE
Quiet Moments
Bath
Spa

with just two proofs of purchase from
any of our four special collector's editions in May.

Harlequin® is sure to make your time special this Mother's Day
with four special collector's editions featuring a short story
PLUS a complete novel packaged together in one volume!

Collection #1 Intrigue abounds in a collection featuring *New York Times*
bestselling author Barbara Delinsky and Kelsey Roberts.

Collection #2 Relationships? Weddings? Children? = *New York Times*
bestselling author Debbie Macomber and Tara Taylor Quinn
at their best!

Collection #3 Escape to the past with *New York Times* bestselling author
Heather Graham and Gayle Wilson.

Collection #4 Go West! With *New York Times* bestselling author
Joan Johnston and Vicki Lewis Thompson!

Plus Special Consumer Campaign!

Each of these four collector's editions will feature a
"FREE QUIET MOMENTS BATH SPA" offer.
See inside book in May for details.

Only from

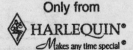

HARLEQUIN®
Makes any time special ®

Don't miss out! Look for this exciting promotion on sale in May 2001,
at your favorite retail outlet.

*Harlequin invites you
to walk down the aisle...*

To honor our year long celebration of weddings, we are offering an exciting opportunity for you to own the Harlequin Bride Doll. Handcrafted in fine bisque porcelain, the wedding doll is dressed for her wedding day in a cream satin gown accented by lace trim. She carries an exquisite traditional bridal bouquet and wears a cathedral-length dotted Swiss veil. Embroidered flowers cascade down her lace overskirt to the scalloped hemline; underneath all is a multi-layered crinoline.

Join us in our celebration of weddings by sending away for your own Harlequin Bride Doll. This doll regularly retails for $74.95 U.S./approx. $108.68 CDN. One doll per household. Requests must be received no later than June 30, 2001. Offer good while quantities of gifts last. Please allow 6-8 weeks for delivery. Offer good in the U.S. and Canada only. Become part of this exciting offer!

**Simply complete the order form and mail to:
"A Walk Down the Aisle"**

IN U.S.A	IN CANADA
P.O. Box 9057	P.O. Box 622
3010 Walden Ave.	Fort Erie, Ontario
Buffalo, NY 14240-9057	L2A 5X3

Enclosed are eight (8) proofs of purchase found on the last page of every specially marked Harlequin series book and $3.75 check or money order (for postage and handling). Please send my Harlequin Bride Doll to:

_____

Name (PLEASE PRINT)

_____

Address   Apt. #

_____

City   State/Prov.   Zip/Postal Code

_____

Account # (if applicable)   **098 KIK DAEW**

HARLEQUIN®
Makes any time special®

Visit us at www.eHarlequin.com

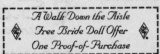

*A Walk Down the Aisle
Free Bride Doll Offer
One Proof-of-Purchase*

PHWDAPOP